Big Trouble
for Roxie

Best Friends

#2

Big Trouble for Roxie

Hilda Stahl

CROSSWAY BOOKS • WHEATON, ILLINOIS
A DIVISION OF GOOD NEWS PUBLISHERS

Dedicated with love to
Dena Hull

Big Trouble for Roxie.

Copyright © 1992 by Word Spinners, Inc.

Published by Crossway Books, a division of
Good News Publishers, 1300 Crescent Street, Wheaton, Illinois 60187.

Cover illustration: Paul Casale

First printing, 1992

Printed in the United States of America

Library of Congress Cataloging-in-Publication Data
Stahl, Hilda.
    Big trouble for Roxie / Hilda Stahl.
        p.   cm.
    Summary: Angry and worried about her grandmother's illness,
Roxie lies to her parents and risks losing her friend Chelsea, but putting
her trust in Jesus helps her repair the damage.
    [1. Christian life—Fiction. 2. Friendship—Fiction.
3. Honesty—Fiction 4. Grandmothers—Fiction.] I. Title.
PZ7.S78244B1 1992   [Fic]—dc20   91-38945
ISBN 0-89107-658-1

00		99		98		97		96		95		94		93		92
15	14	13	12	11	10	9	8	7	6	5	4	3	2	1

Contents

1

The Flying W Ranch

With a great flourish Roxie handed the notebook to Kathy Aber. They had just had their *King's Kids* meeting in her yard under the giant maple tree. All four of them were dressed in shorts and T-shirts. "Be sure to write everything down so I can read it when I get back from my vacation at The Flying W Ranch," said Roxie, once again stressing the *Flying W Ranch*. She was secretary of their group, and Kathy was vice president. Kathy filled in whenever it was necessary.

"I'll print the notes to be sure everyone can read them," said Kathy as she opened the notebook to the notes Roxie had made at today's meeting. Roxie's handwriting was large, and the notes filled three pages.

"I wish I was going with you, Roxie," said Hannah Shigwam with a long sigh. She was the treasurer because she was good in math. "I've never even touched a horse in my whole life!"

"I rode when we lived in Oklahoma," said Chelsea McCrea. She was the president because she'd thought up the group when she'd built up a huge long-distance phone bill by calling her best friend in Oklahoma many times. She was paying her father back by working odd jobs in the neighborhood. Many of the other kids in The Ravines, the subdivision where they lived, wanted jobs too, so she'd let them join. She called the group *King's Kids* because the four leaders were all Christians and belonged to the King of kings, Jesus.

"I'll think of you girls while I'm riding," said Roxie, sounding very smug. She was glad she was going to the ranch. She'd never had anything exciting to talk about in her entire life, but after spending two weeks on a dude ranch she'd have plenty to say for months and months.

"We aren't going on a vacation," said Chelsea as she twisted a strand of long red hair around her finger. "Dad can't leave his new job. But we did get to visit Lake Michigan last weekend. It looked like a giant ocean to me."

Roxie wanted to make fun of Chelsea for making such a big deal out of visiting Lake Michigan, but she kept her mouth closed. She'd promised to be nice to Chelsea even when she didn't feel like it. Chelsea had let her join *King's Kids*, and for that

Roxie was thankful. Chelsea was the only one in the group who hadn't been born and raised in Michigan. The rest of them had grown up swimming at the lake several weekends during the summer when it was warm enough or when the waves weren't too high.

Roxie glanced at the other three girls. She knew they were best friends with each other. It made her feel left out. They were her friends, but not *best* friends. Sometimes she didn't even like Chelsea, and she knew Chelsea didn't always like her. Both Kathy and Hannah loved Chelsea and told her all of their secrets. Roxie just couldn't bring herself to tell any of them her secrets. She'd never had a best friend in her entire life. Rob, Chelsea's brother, was almost a best friend, but lately he'd been spending more time with Nick Rand—he lived a few blocks away on Hornbeam—than with her. But even that didn't bother her today. She was going to The Flying W! Nobody else here was doing anything that exciting and probably never had.

Kathy jumped up, holding Roxie's notebook tight against her. She was the only one in the group who lived outside The Ravines—on Kennedy Street. "I have to get home before 3 to watch Megan."

"Be sure to call each person to remind them of their jobs," said Roxie. She always made sure she called each *King's Kid* to give him or her the location and description for his or her particular job. "We don't want any unhappy customers."

Kathy lifted her chin high, and her blonde curls bounced. "I will do exactly what I'm supposed to do, Roxie Shoulders!"

"Don't fight, girls," said Hannah.

"We won't," said Roxie. She was in too good a mood to fight with anyone. She'd waited three years to go to The Flying W Ranch. Nothing was going to ruin it for her. She said good-bye to Kathy and watched her ride away on her bike.

Hannah said, "I have to go home too." She looked across the street where she lived, then turned back to Roxie. "Have fun on your vacation."

"Thanks," said Roxie, smiling.

"I'll call you later, Hannah," said Chelsea as Hannah ran across the street.

Hannah stopped near the large rock in her front yard, waved, then ran across the green lawn and into the house.

Just then Gracie, a small brown dog, ran into Roxie's yard and right over to the flower garden near the front of the house.

"Get out of there, Gracie!" shouted Chelsea, jumping up.

"I'll get her," Roxie said grimly as she broke off a switch from the maple tree. She raced across her yard, her black hair bouncing on her head. Just as

Roxie reached Gracie, Chelsea grabbed for the switch.

"Stop that!" Roxie cried, jerking away from Chelsea. Roxie leaped toward Gracie, the switch held high.

"Run, Gracie!" cried Chelsea as she chased Gracie away.

"She needs to be whipped!" Roxie snapped.

Her cheeks flaming as red as her hair, Chelsea turned on Roxie. "You said you wouldn't hit Gracie again!"

"I'll do anything to her I want if she gets in Mom's flowers!" cried Roxie, her dark eyes flashing. "Mom wants to win the PRETTIEST FLOWERS CONTEST again this year, and I'm going to help her do it!"

"Not by beating a dog!" Chelsea said, her chest rising and falling.

"Gracie won't obey unless you spank her," said Roxie sharply. "You'll see."

Chelsea shook her head. "I won't hit Gracie no matter what!"

Roxie shook the switch at Chelsea. "Mom hired you to tend the flowers while we're gone. It'll be all your fault if Gracie tears them up!"

Sparks flew from Chelsea's blue eyes. "I won't hit Gracie!"

"Oh, just go home where you belong!"

Chelsea hesitated, then ran home.

Roxie stamped her foot. "I won't even tell her

about my vacation, no matter how much she begs."
Roxie walked to her house and flung the switch
down on the steps. "I don't care if we're never best
friends!"

Later Roxie stood in front of the full-length
mirror on her bedroom door and squinted until she
could barely see herself. She tried not to see her red
shorts and bright yellow T-shirt. If she pretended
hard enough, she could see a white cowgirl hat on
her head, blue hand-tooled boots on her feet, and a
blue-and-white plaid western shirt with just-right
faded jeans on her body. That's exactly how she'd
dress during the two weeks at The Flying W Dude
Ranch outside Titanka, Wyoming. If she could dress
like that now in Middle Lake, Michigan, at The
Ravines, she would. But too many people would
laugh at her. And that she couldn't take.

With a loud sigh she whirled away from her
mirror. Why couldn't she be like her sister Lacy?
Nothing embarrassed *her*. Not even Dad when he
wore his paint-stained overalls with the rip in the
knee to the grocery store.

Suddenly Roxie had a terrible thought. What if
Dad took his overalls with him to the ranch? No
cowboy would ever dress in overalls!

She ran to her bedroom window and looked
down on the street below. She'd watch for Dad to
get home from his construction job, then beg him to
leave his overalls home. This year's vacation was her

choice, so maybe he'd listen to her just to make her happy.

"He'd better," she said grimly. She leaned against the window and waited.

2

The Phone Call

Roxie turned from her bedroom window with a frown. The phone had already rung five times. Why wasn't anyone answering it? She knew Dad wasn't home yet because she'd been watching for him. Maybe Mom wasn't back from buying Faye a swimsuit for the vacation. Faye was four, and she'd worn her other swimsuit out by wearing it while playing in the sandbox.

"Answer the phone, Lacy," Roxie shouted through her bedroom door. Lacy didn't answer. She was sixteen, and she loved answering the phone. She must not be home. The phone rang again. "Eli, answer the phone!" He was fifteen, and he answered only if Lacy didn't. It usually wasn't for him, but he kept hoping. He didn't answer, so he must be gone too.

On the eighth ring Roxie ran to the extension in the hallway outside Lacy's room and grabbed the receiver. "Hello," she said, sounding hurried. She didn't want to stay on the phone and miss Dad.

"Roxann! I was so afraid you'd already left on your trip. Is your mom there?"

"I guess not, Grandma." Grandma Potter was the only person who ever called her by her full name. "I better go, Grandma. I got a lot to do yet."

"Wait, Roxann!" Grandma sounded close to tears.

Roxie's heart jerked strangely. "What's wrong, Grandma?"

"Nothing to worry you about, Roxann. Take down this number and have your mom call me right away. Don't forget. It's very important."

Roxie trembled. If Mom called Grandma instead of packing for the trip, they'd get a late start. Grandma lived across town. They'd lived next door to her until they'd moved into The Ravines two years ago. Roxie twisted the white phone cord around her finger. Mom might even decide to run over to see Grandma before they left. Maybe she shouldn't give Mom the message. She pushed the pencil back in the tiny drawer in the tiny desk that held the phone, the phone book, and a small notepad. She didn't write down the number. An icy band tightened around her heart. "I have to go now, Grandma." Could Grandma hear the guilt in her voice?

"I love you, Roxann," said Grandma hoarsely.

Roxie gripped the receiver tighter. She'd always known Grandma loved her, but Grandma usually didn't say the words. "I love you, too, Grandma," said Roxie in a rush. "See you when we get back."

"See you," said Grandma.

Roxie hung up before Grandma could say anything else. Roxie's legs suddenly felt so weak she didn't know if she could make it back to her bedroom. This was a secret she could never tell Chelsea, Hannah, or Kathy. They'd say she was bad. They'd say Jesus wouldn't want her to keep the message from Mom. Roxie pressed her lips tightly together. She did do it! And she was glad!

Weakly she leaned against the window to watch for Dad. To her horror he stood in the yard dressed in dirty overalls. His dark hair was standing on end like he'd just pulled off his ugly bright pink-and-red cap. He owned the construction company where he worked, but he always filled in if they were short of help. He never came home looking clean and handsome in a business suit like Chelsea's dad. Even Hannah's dad wore dress clothes to work. Why couldn't her dad be like the other dads at The Ravines? None of them told dumb jokes, then laughed so hard the whole neighborhood could hear them. It didn't bother her dad if the whole world was watching when he kissed Mom. He wrestled with Eli right out in the yard as if he was a boy too.

How could she get him to act right at The Flying W so she wouldn't be embarrassed by him?

She ran downstairs and met Dad in the yard. He smelled like sweat and paint thinner. Before she could stop him, he picked her up and swung her around as if she were four years old like Faye instead of twelve.

"You're looking as pretty as usual, Roxie," said Dad. "You're looking more and more like your mom every day."

Roxie scowled. She didn't want to look like Mom *ever*. Mom was almost twenty pounds over-weight and didn't even care!

"Are you ready for The Flying W?" asked Dad, ruffling Roxie's short dark hair.

"Yes." She looked intently up at him. "Are you?"

"Sure am! Take me to them horses!" Dad grabbed a rake leaning against the garage, straddled it, and rode it around the yard, yelling, "Get 'um up, Scout! Hi ho, Silver, away!"

Roxie groaned and wanted to sink out of sight. She darted a look around to make sure nobody saw her dad acting so childish. She breathed a sigh of relief when she didn't see anyone watching. She wanted to tell her dad to stop, but she knew it wouldn't do any good.

Finally Dad leaned the rake against the side of the garage and brushed the seat of his pants as if he had been riding. "That was some ride. I thought I'd get bucked off for a while, but I made it."

"Dad . . ." Roxie said with a frown.

Dad laughed. "Sorry. Did you want a ride? Go right ahead." He held the rake out to her, and she scowled harder. He chuckled as he propped the rake back in place. "Don't tell me you're too grown-up to ride. How'll you manage at The Flying W?"

"They have real horses there," said Roxie stiffly.

Dad looked at the rake with a slight frown. "Real horses? Is that why I couldn't find the stirrups on your saddle, Rake?" He slapped his leg and laughed harder.

Roxie flushed to the roots of her hair. Why wouldn't Dad grow up? "Let's go inside so we can talk," she said.

Dad followed her through the garage to the door leading into the laundry room. He dropped his cap on the hook at the back door. Once they were in the kitchen he said, "What's so important?"

Roxie took a deep breath. "It's your overalls, Dad."

He looked down at the dirty overalls, then shrugged. "They get dirty. That's life."

"Will you please leave them home when we go on vacation? Cowboys don't wear overalls."

"You don't say." Dad winked at her. "Sure, I'll leave 'em home. Can I wear my jeans?"

"Of course! But not the ones with paint smeared on the leg."

"I'll leave 'em home too. It's your say on this vacation."

Roxie breathed a sigh of relief. Every year they took turns choosing where they'd go on vacation. Finally her turn had come, and nothing was going to ruin it. "And don't wear your caps."

"I don't have a cowboy hat."

"We could buy one for you."

"And for all of us?" asked Dad with a twinkle in his eye.

"Yes!" cried Roxie.

Dad kissed her flushed cheek. "We'll have to settle on cheap straw hats then. It's not in our vacation budget to buy the real thing."

"Straw hats are okay."

This was more than she'd hoped for.

Just then Mom and Faye walked in the back door with their arms full of bags. Mom wore beige slacks and a flowered blouse. Her brown hair was streaked with gray at the temples. She was a year older than Dad, but it never bothered her. Roxie had decided years ago she'd never marry a man younger than herself.

"I bought jeans for all of us," said Mom as Dad helped her.

Roxie frowned as she helped Faye. Didn't Mom know cowboys didn't ever wear new jeans?

Faye pulled a red sucker out of her mouth. She had blue eyes like Dad's. "I don't want to ride a horse, Roxie. It might step on me."

"It won't," said Roxie. "The horses are well trained. They know not to step on little girls."

Faye lifted her chin and her eyes flashed. "I'm not a little girl! I am four. And I am going to start school this year."

Roxie bit back a sharp answer. They'd already told Faye a million times she couldn't start school until next year when she turned five. But she wouldn't believe them.

"I bought plenty of film for the camera," said Mom as she pulled film from a bag. "This year we'd better remember to take the camera." Last year they'd had lots of film, but had left the camera home on the counter.

"I'll make sure it gets packed," said Roxie. She wanted pictures of herself riding a horse and hanging out with the cowboys and cowgirls at the ranch.

Lacy ran through the back door with Eli close behind her. "I'm home! Did anybody call?"

Just then the phone rang, and Roxie jumped. She flushed as she thought about Grandma's message. Maybe she was calling back. But it was a business call for Dad, and Roxie breathed easier.

For the next hour as they loaded the station wagon she held her breath each time the phone rang.

All the calls were for Lacy. Her friends wanted to make sure to say good-bye.

Lacy flipped back her long auburn hair and laughed breathlessly. "I don't know if I want to leave," she said. "Two weeks is a long time to be away from everybody."

Roxie frowned at Lacy. The others were outdoors at the station wagon. "You know you have to go. Mom wouldn't leave you here alone."

Lacy tugged her extra-long T-shirt down over her jeans. "I'm old enough to stay alone."

"I know," said Roxie. She was willing to say anything to keep Lacy happy. "But you'll have fun at The Flying W."

"Not as much fun as we had at the beach," said Lacy as the phone rang again. With a breathless laugh she answered it.

Roxie waited with her stomach in a tight knot. Once again it was for Lacy. Roxie ran outdoors to the others with the last load of her things.

Eli took the luggage from her and pushed it into place on the rack on top of the station wagon. He was strong from working out. He stepped back and pushed his glasses up on his nose. "Nothing else will fit, Dad," he said.

"Then let's cover it and tie the ropes in place," said Dad.

Roxie locked her icy fingers together as she watched Dad and Eli secure the luggage rack. Soon they'd be on their way. Dad said they'd drive about four hours tonight, then stop at a motel and continue the trip tomorrow. The day after that, they would be at The Flying W Ranch. Nothing would stop them now!

Lacy stuck her head out the door and called, "Mom, Grandma's on the phone."

Roxie's heart zoomed to her feet. She wanted to grab Mom and keep her from running to the phone.

"Give her my love," called Dad as Mom ran inside.

Roxie rolled her eyes and bit her tongue to keep from screaming out in frustration. It was almost seven o'clock, and Dad had said they'd leave right at 7. It stayed light out until almost 9:30. Grandma might make them so late that Dad would decide to wait until morning to leave. Roxie glanced at Dad. He'd changed into loose-fitting jeans and a nice blue-and-white pullover shirt. Even his hair was combed neatly. He passed her test. If she watched him closely enough during vacation, maybe he wouldn't wear or do anything to embarrass her.

"You guys go check one last time to make sure you didn't leave anything important behind," said Dad as he headed for the house. "I want to see what Grandma wants."

Roxie ran after Dad. She wanted to hear everything. Maybe Grandma wouldn't mention that she'd called earlier. Roxie's mouth felt bone-dry as she stopped just inside the kitchen door. Mom's face was pale, and tears stood in her eyes. Roxie swallowed hard. Was something wrong with Grandma after all?

Finally Mom hung up. She groped for Dad's hand, and he pulled her close.

"What is it, Ilene?" he asked softly.

"Mom's in the hospital, Burt," she said with a catch in her voice.

Roxie sagged against the door frame. The hospital!

"She had to go in for tests, and she has to stay in for a few days."

"We'll unpack the car," said Dad.

Roxie leaped forward with a cry. "No! What about our vacation?"

"We'll go after Grandma's out of the hospital," said Dad, looking over Mom's head at Roxie.

"We can't leave until we know Grandma's all right," said Mom with her face buried against Dad's chest.

Roxie turned away, her face dark with anger. How dare they postpone the trip! It wasn't fair! What if something else happened and they never got to go at all?

3

The Bad News

Tears burning her eyes, Roxie wandered around her yard while she waited to hear from Mom and Dad about Grandma. They'd been gone over an hour already.

"Roxie!" cried Chelsea in surprise as she ran to Roxie. "How come you're still here?"

"What d' you care?" snapped Roxie.

Chelsea stared in surprise at Roxie. "How come you're mad at me? What did I do to you?"

"Can't you learn to talk like everybody else?" Roxie hated hearing Chelsea's Oklahoma accent, especially tonight.

Chelsea's blue eyes flashed, and her cheeks turned red enough to make her freckles blur together. She headed back home, then stopped. "Roxie, I know something happened to keep you from leaving on your vacation. I'm sorry you couldn't go."

"Don't be nice to me!" Roxie struggled to keep back her tears. But one plopped off her cheek and landed on her sneaker anyway.

"I have to be nice," said Chelsea. "We signed the Best Friends Pact, remember? We promised to be kind to each other."

Roxie remembered, but it didn't mean anything to her because she didn't feel like a best friend to the girls and they didn't feel like they were to her.

"Tell me why you're so sad," said Chelsea softly.

Roxie shook her head.

Chelsea sighed. "Should I call Hannah and Kathy? They'd want to come help you too."

"They wouldn't come," said Roxie.

"Yes, they would."

Roxie bit her lip and shook her head. "Don't get them."

"Then let me help," said Chelsea.

Roxie looked off across the street. Hannah's little sisters were laughing and playing in their front yard. Music drifted out from another house. Roxie took a deep breath. "My grandma's in the hospital, and we can't go on vacation until she's out."

"I'm sorry," said Chelsea.

Roxie peeked through her dark lashes at Chelsea to see if she meant what she said. She did! A few more tears slipped down Roxie's cheeks. "Mom is scared something really bad is wrong with

Grandma." Roxie couldn't bring herself to admit she'd kept Grandma's phone call from Mom.

"We'll pray for her," said Chelsea.

"Really?"

"We promised to pray for each other."

"I forgot," whispered Roxie.

"You and I can pray right now."

Roxie glanced quickly around. "Here? Now?" What if someone saw them?

"Sure. It doesn't matter to Jesus where we are when we pray." Chelsea reached for Roxie's hand.

Roxie jumped back. "You can pray when you go home, and I'll pray at bedtime. That's when I pray." Unless she forgot, but she didn't tell Chelsea that.

"I'll call Hannah and Kathy so they can pray too," Chelsea said as she started back to her yard. She stopped just inside her yard and turned back to Roxie. "Jesus answers prayer, Roxie. He'll take care of your grandma."

Roxie nodded slightly. She'd never been able to talk to Jesus as if he was her friend like the other girls did. But she didn't tell Chelsea that either. There were many things she couldn't tell the others. That's why she knew she and they weren't best friends. Best friends shared everything.

Just then her dad and mom pulled in the driveway and parked outside the garage. The sound of the car engine sounded extra-loud to Roxie. She ran to them. As they got out of the car she said, "How's Grandma?"

Mom sighed heavily and shook her head. Dad hurried around the car and slipped his arm around Mom, almost like he was holding her up.

"We'll talk inside," said Dad. He looked very serious, not his usual laughing self.

Roxie's stomach cramped as she followed them into the living room, where Lacy and Eli were watching TV. Faye was asleep on the floor with a multicolored afghan over her that Grandma had knitted years ago. Without a word Eli clicked off the TV. The room seemed very quiet. The smell of buttered popcorn that Eli had popped earlier hung in the air.

Roxie sank to the floor and pressed her back tight against the couch. She stared down at the carpet. She was afraid to hear what Dad was going to say.

Mom sat in her special chair, and Dad perched on the arm of it, his hand on Mom's shoulder.

"Grandma is being checked for cancer," said Dad solemnly.

Lacy gasped. "Cancer! But she could die!"

Mom burst into tears.

Roxie locked her icy hands around her knees. She'd kept Grandma's message from Mom! What if they'd gone to Wyoming, then Grandma had died?

It was too terrible to think about. Guilt at what she'd done burned inside her.

"The doctor will know in a few days," said Dad. "I'm going to call a few people who believe in prayer so they'll pray for Grandma."

Roxie wished she'd let Chelsea pray right in the yard when she'd wanted to.

"Could we all pray together right now?" whispered Mom.

Roxie flushed. Their family had never prayed together as long as she could remember. She knew Chelsea's family did, and so did Kathy's and Hannah's.

Dad cleared his throat. "I think we should." He looked at Lacy, Eli, and Roxie. "Kids, come here and we'll hold hands and pray. I'm not too sure what to say, but I'll do my best."

Slowly Roxie walked to Mom and Dad. She stood between Eli and Lacy. Eli's hand felt hard and Lacy's soft. Roxie bowed her head and closed her eyes. It felt strange to pray right in the middle of the living room.

"Lord God, You have . . . promised to . . . help us," Dad prayed. "Grandma needs Your help right now . . . And so do we. Keep Grandma safe from cancer. And comfort us so we're not afraid. In Jesus' name, Amen."

Without looking at anyone, Roxie pulled away

from Eli and Lacy. She was thankful the prayer was short.

Mom blew her nose. "Thank you, Burt," she said softly.

"You're welcome." He cleared his throat. "I'd better call The Flying W and let them know we can't make it right now."

Roxie bit her lip. She didn't deserve to go at all because of the terrible secret she'd kept from Mom! Roxie shuddered just thinking about what could've happened if they'd left on their trip without knowing Grandma was even in the hospital.

Slowly Roxie walked to her bedroom. She stood at the window and looked at the lights streaming from the houses around her. What would Chelsea and Hannah and Kathy think of her if they found out what she'd done? She frowned and knotted her fists. They'd never find out! She'd make sure of that.

After her shower Roxie pulled on her lightweight blue pajamas and slipped between her sheets. The night-light in the hallway and the streetlight outdoors kept her room from being dark. She was glad because tonight she just couldn't sleep in the dark. Maybe she wouldn't be able to sleep at all.

Mom walked in just as she did every night and kissed Roxie good night. "Try not to worry," whispered Mom.

Roxie couldn't speak around the lump in her

throat. Would Mom hate her if she knew the truth? "Will Grandma die?"

Tears slipped down Mom's cheeks. "I don't want her to. She's too young!"

She seemed old to Roxie, but she didn't say that.

"We'll keep praying for her," said Mom as she brushed away her tears. She stayed a few more minutes, then walked down the hall to Eli's room.

Roxie quietly slipped from her bed and knelt beside it. It was the way she prayed when she remembered to. She folded her hands, but no words came. All she could think about was the secret she'd kept from Mom because of her own selfishness. Finally she climbed back in bed, but it was a long time before she fell asleep.

The next day she ran over to Chelsea's house and knocked on her back door. It was early, but she knew Chelsea would be up and getting ready to go to work at whatever job she had.

Rob opened the door and let her in. He had curly auburn hair and blue eyes and was wearing jeans and a T-shirt. "Hi," he said, smiling.

Roxie felt better just seeing him. He was the first person who had ever liked her even though he knew she wasn't perfect. "Do you have a job today?"

"Yes. Mowing a couple of lawns." Rob

frowned slightly. "Hey, you're supposed to be gone."

"I know." She hesitantly told him about her grandma.

"I'll pray for her while I'm mowing the lawns," said Rob. He picked up his cap. "I got to go now. I hear Chel coming. See you later."

"See you," said Roxie weakly. Would Jesus listen to Rob pray while he was mowing the lawn?

Chelsea ran into the kitchen and stopped short. "Roxie! You're still here! What about your grandma?"

"She . . . might . . . have . . . cancer," whispered Roxie.

"God works miracles. We'll keep praying for your grandma," said Chelsea. "What about your vacation?"

"We have to wait until Grandma's out of the hospital." Roxie bit her lower lip. "I came to see if you have a job I can do. I don't want to sit around the house and wait."

Chelsea shook her head. "Only five people called for workers today, and they're all assigned. Sorry."

"What about next week?"

"All assigned. But we might get another call. If no one else can take it, we'll give it to you."

"I could take care of Mom's flowers since I'll be home. Then you won't have to."

Chelsea shook her head. "I have to have that job to pay for my phone bill. Besides, your mom especially wants me to take care of them because of the contest. She knows I'm good with flowers."

"So am I!" cried Roxie.

"Not as good as I am," said Chelsea sharply.

Roxie whirled around and slammed out of the house. She should've known Chelsea wasn't really her friend. Hannah and Kathy probably weren't either. She'd forget about the Best Friends Pact and about *King's Kids* too. She'd stay home and watch TV forever!

$$\boxed{4}$$

Best Friends

Roxie punched her pillow, then plopped down on her bed. The morning seemed ten days long.

Just then Lacy poked her head in the door. "Your friend Hannah Shigwam is downstairs, Roxie."

"I don't have friends."

Lacy frowned. "Stop feeling sorry for yourself. She's waiting in the living room. Get down there and see her *now*."

Roxie knew better than to argue with Lacy when she used that tone of voice. "Oh, all right! But she isn't my friend!" Roxie walked slowly downstairs. The smell of morning coffee still lingered in the air. Music blared from Eli's room. Roxie hesitated outside the living room, then walked in. Hannah sat on the couch waiting for her. She wore blue shorts and a white T-shirt with orange and red flowers on the front. Her thick dark hair was held back from her face with an orange band. She jumped up when she saw Roxie.

"I'm sorry about your grandma," Hannah said.

"I didn't expect you to come," Roxie said stiffly. She didn't know how to act.

"Me and my family prayed for her," said Hannah.

Roxie started to say something mean, then changed her mind. "Thanks."

"Lacy said your mom and dad are at the hospital with your grandma."

Roxie nodded. She wished Hannah would leave.

"I memorized a Bible verse this morning."

Roxie bit her bottom lip. In their Best Friends Pact they'd agreed to learn a Bible verse every day. So far she hadn't learned even one. She'd signed the Best Friends Pact only because the others expected her to do it. They'd all agreed they'd stick together no matter what, help each other at all times, pray for each other, learn a Bible verse a day, and do good deeds. She didn't keep any of the agreements, and she didn't care who knew it. Well, maybe she sort of didn't want anyone to know.

"It's Psalm 46, verse 1," said Hannah with a slow smile. "'God is our refuge and strength, a very present help in trouble.'"

Roxie didn't know what to say. She'd never

think to tell a Bible verse to someone to help that person out.

"It means God will keep you safe and give you strength and He'll help you when you're in trouble."

"Oh," said Roxie. She had never heard that before. But then she didn't listen in Sunday school or church. Everything always seemed so boring. The verse did sound good, and it made her feel a little better to know God really would help. But would He really help *her*? Why would He when she was so bad?

Hannah started for the door. "I guess I'd better go. I have three jobs to do today."

Roxie's heart leaped. Here was her chance. "I could do one of them!"

Hannah shook her head. "They're short jobs, and the people asked for me. Sorry. See ya later."

"See ya," said Roxie. Her shoulders drooped, and she felt like crying because she didn't have anything to do. A job would keep her mind off Grandma and even off herself and how bad she was.

Just as Hannah left, Kathy dropped her bike outside the door and ran inside. Her blonde curls bobbed on her head. She wore red shorts and a light pink T-shirt that had three red flowers with green leaves.

"Hi!" said Kathy, smiling brightly.

Roxie wanted to tell her to leave, but she forced a smile and said, "Hi."

"I prayed for your family and your grandma," said Kathy.

"Thanks," said Roxie weakly. Was she the only one who signed the Pact that wasn't keeping the promises?

"How is your grandma?" asked Kathy as she pushed back a strand of blonde hair.

Roxie shrugged. "I don't know. Dad said he'd call when they know anything."

"I wish I could do something to make you feel better," said Kathy, reaching out to Roxie.

"You can't," snapped Roxie as she jumped out of Kathy's reach.

"I wanted to cheer you up before I go to work," said Kathy.

"You don't need to," said Roxie. Just then a great idea popped into her head. If she had her secretary book back from Kathy, she'd see where the jobs were and she could get there and start working before the persons assigned arrived. She'd say the others couldn't make it and she was filling in. A shiver ran down her spine. She forced a smile. "Now that I'm going to be home I'll take over my job as secretary."

"You don't have to," Kathy said, shaking her head. "I don't mind doing it at all. You should stay with your family and help encourage them and not even think about working."

"I want the book back!" said Roxie sharply. "I am the secretary, and I can do my own job!"

Kathy looked down at the floor, then at Roxie. "I guess you can," said Kathy. "But I already called the kids who are working the next few days. You won't have anything to do."

Roxie shrugged. Should she try to do the jobs before the others arrived? Her stomach knotted at the terrible thought. Could she really be so mean? She was mean enough to keep Grandma's phone call from Mom, so she probably was bad enough to take jobs that weren't hers. But how could she stand herself if she did such an awful thing? In a rush she said, "I changed my mind. You keep the book until I get back from vacation . . . If I really get to go," she added in a whisper.

"You will!" said Kathy, nodding. "We prayed!"

Roxie bit her lip. How did Kathy know for sure that God answered prayer?

"Jesus loves you, Roxie," said Kathy. "He wants the very best for your life."

Roxie didn't know how Kathy could speak so openly about Jesus. How did she know so much about Him? Roxie locked her hands together behind her back. It made her feel funny to have Kathy talk about Jesus that way. She stepped back from Kathy and wished she'd leave. Suddenly she wished she had taken the book so she'd have something to occupy her time. Now what would she do all day long?

"I know!" Kathy cried, holding her hand out to Roxie.

"What?" asked Roxie suspiciously.

"You can take my job for today!"

Roxie frowned. "Is it a rotten job?"

"No!"

"Then why would you give up your job for me?"

"Because we're friends! We promised to be kind and helpful to people and especially to each other," Kathy said, smiling. "I thought maybe it would make you feel better if you had something to do."

Roxie didn't know what to say. "What job is it?" she asked stiffly.

"Sweeping out two garages—Mrs. Greene's and Mrs. VanDorn's."

"They pay a lot more than we ask," said Roxie, looking at Kathy as if she'd lost her mind for giving the jobs up so easily.

"You'd do the same for me," said Kathy.

Tears burned the backs of Roxie's eyes. She wouldn't do the same! She couldn't imagine Kathy giving up jobs for her.

"Do you want the jobs?" asked Kathy. "If you're too upset to take them, I'll do them. I really thought it might help if you had something to keep you busy while you're waiting to hear about your grandma."

"If I take the job, I won't share the money with you," Roxie said sharply.

Kathy shrugged. "I wouldn't expect you to."

Roxie narrowed her eyes. Was Kathy for real? "Are you doing it because you feel sorry for me?"

"Well . . . Yes."

"Then I don't want the job!" Roxie lifted her chin and narrowed her brown eyes. She hated to have others feel sorry for her! "You don't have to feel sorry for me or do anything for me."

Kathy's cheeks turned pink, and her hazel eyes sparked with anger. "I have been trying to keep my temper, Roxie Shoulders, but you make it very hard! I wouldn't give you the jobs now if you begged for them!" She whirled around and marched out of the living room and out the front door, slamming it hard behind her.

Roxie plopped on the couch and burst into tears. Why was she always so mean to people? What was wrong with her?

Just then Faye ran into the living room. She sat down beside Roxie and pushed a book into her hands. "Teach me to read, Roxie."

"Get away from me!" Flushing, Roxie dried her tears. She hated to cry in front of anyone.

"I won't!" Faye flipped back her long, light

brown ponytails. "I have to learn to read so I can start school!"

"We told you a million times you can't start school this year!"

"Well, I am going to! So there!" Faye held the book in her lap and leaned over it. "I will teach myself to read."

"Go right ahead!"

Faye stared at the first word for a long time. Finally she flung the book to the floor. "You're mean!"

"You're a baby!"

"I am not! I'm four years old."

"You're such a baby that you have to sleep on a cot in Mom and Dad's room." Roxie saw the pain flash in Faye's eyes, but she was past caring. "You're such a baby that you're too scared to sleep in your own room." She was too. They'd finally turned it into a guest room. "You'll never be old enough to start school until you can sleep in your own room."

Faye burst into tears and ran from the room.

Anger at herself raged through Roxie. What was wrong with her? Why had she hurt her sweet little sister Faye?

With a strangled cry Roxie ran outdoors. She stopped short when she saw Chelsea quietly working in Mom's flower garden. Chelsea looked so nice and sweet that all of Roxie's anger turned toward her. "I said I'd do that!" screamed Roxie, racing across the yard toward Chelsea.

Chelsea jumped up, her eyes wide with alarm.

"You leave those flowers alone, Chelsea McCrea! I will take care of them!"

"No!" Chelsea shook her head hard. "You can't and you know it. Your mom told *me* to."

Roxie dropped to her knees at the flower bed, jerked the plants right out of the ground, and flung them into the grass.

Chelsea grabbed Roxie's arm and tried to pull her away from the flowers. "Stop that! Roxie, stop that right now!"

Roxie pushed Chelsea away and yanked another row of flowers out. Suddenly she turned on Chelsea. "Get out of my yard right now—and don't come back!"

"But the flowers!"

"I'll tell Mom you got mad and did this," said Roxie with her eyes narrowed and her fists on her hips. "And she'll believe me!"

Giant tears welled up in Chelsea's eyes and slipped down her cheeks. She turned and slowly walked away.

Roxie dropped to the grass and covered her face with her hands. This was the worst thing she'd ever done in her life. Now what was she going to do?

Terrible sobs tore through her throat. Tears soaked her hands as she wept in agony.

5

Ilene Shoulders's Flowers

Roxie took a deep shuddering breath, then slowly wiped away her tears. She looked at the destruction she'd done to her mom's flowers, and her heart sank. What could she do? Mom would be heart-broken if she couldn't win the PRETTIEST FLOWERS CONTEST. Roxie remembered how Chelsea had replaced the flowers the time Gracie had torn them up. She'd do the same thing now!

Carefully Roxie buried the plants back in the flower bed. She filled the watering can and watered each plant just the way Chelsea had done it before. Most of the plants drooped weakly. The flower bed looked ugly with clods of dirt lying here and there. Some of the flowers were buried too deep in the ground and others too high up. Her heart sank. She smelled the soil on her hands and saw the dirt under her fingernails. With a loud sigh she worked the ground again and tried to make it look smooth the

HILDA STAHL

way it had before. Her hands got muddy from
working in the wet ground. She rubbed them on the
grass, but couldn't get them clean.

She glanced toward Chelsea's house. Should
she ask Chelsea to come help her? She shook her
head hard. It would be too embarrassing to beg
Chelsea to take care of the flowers after what she'd
done. She'd never be able to face Chelsea again.
Roxie sighed heavily. Chelsea had probably told
Hannah and Kathy what had happened. All three of
them would be mad at her.

A car drove past, and Roxie jumped. What
would she say to Mom when she saw how terrible
the flower bed looked? Could she really say Chelsea
had done it? She didn't want to, but she didn't want
Mom mad at her either. She'd have to lie. Her stomach knotted, and a black cloud settled over her.
Could she really be so bad? Was she ever nice? She
thought of the time she'd helped Chelsea feel better
when her best friend in Oklahoma had broken up
with her. She'd been nice then. Maybe that would be
the last nice thing she'd do in her entire life.

Slowly Roxie walked inside and washed her
hands. She watched the dirt run down the drain. But
she still felt dirty inside with dirt that couldn't be
washed away with water.

"Where's my protein drink?" shouted Eli from
the kitchen.

Roxie hung the towel in place and walked into

the kitchen. "It's probably right where you left it." Eli was determined to be strong enough to make the first string on the football team. He did a regular workout program down in the basement where his weights were set up and drank his special protein drink daily.

"It's not," said Eli as he pushed his glasses up on his nose.

Just then Faye walked in. She opened a cupboard under the counter and pulled out Eli's protein drink.

"Hey! What're you doing with that, Faye?" asked Eli, grabbing it from her.

"I'm trying to grow so I will be big enough to start school," said Faye, trying to grab it back.

"It won't work," said Roxie, shaking her head.

Faye wrinkled her nose at Roxie, then turned back to Eli. "Please let me have some."

"You can have part of it," Eli said as he poured milk in the blender.

The kitchen door slammed, and Mom snapped, "Roxie, what happened to my flowers?"

Roxie desperately wanted to tell the truth, but she just couldn't. "Chelsea took care of them. You hired her. Remember?" Every word almost choked Roxie. Every word made her feel dirtier and dirtier.

"I'll have a word with that girl!" Mom started back out the door, but Dad caught her arm.

"You're too upset to speak to her now," said Dad.

"I certainly won't pay her," said Mom, shaking her head.

Roxie gasped. Chelsea was counting on the money to help pay her phone bill.

"And you're tired after being at the hospital most of the day," said Dad. "I want you to sit down while I make you a sandwich. Then you're going to take a nap before we go back."

"All right," said Mom, sinking onto a kitchen chair.

Roxie breathed a sigh of relief. She didn't want Mom to ask Chelsea about the flowers. "Since we're going to be home, let me take care of the flowers," Roxie said.

Mom threw up her hands. "All right! I can't understand what happened though. Chelsea has a green thumb. But it certainly doesn't show in that front flower bed!"

Roxie turned away to hide her crimson face.

"How's Grandma?" asked Lacy from the dining room doorway.

"She's resting well," said Mom.

"The doctor hasn't found anything serious," said Dad. "Thank God!"

Roxie grew very quiet. Was it possible that prayer did make a difference? She knew about asking Jesus to be her Savior, but she thought that was all there was to it. She'd ask Kathy and Hannah and Chelsea to tell her more. She bit back a whimper. She couldn't ask them. She'd made sure of that!

While Mom rested in her room, Roxie worked on the flower bed until she felt like she couldn't do another thing. But it still looked bad. She watered them again. Two plants fell right over, and her heart sank. She propped the plants back up, but the ground was too wet. She moved the plants to a spot that wasn't quite so wet, and they stayed in place. But their tops drooped, and she began to whimper.

After Mom and Dad returned to the hospital Roxie paced her bedroom while she tried to figure a way to make the flower bed look good again. She wanted to ask Chelsea, but she couldn't.

Just then Faye walked past the bedroom door, her arms full of toys.

Roxie stepped to the doorway and watched Faye go into the spare room. "What are you doing, Faye?"

Faye walked into the hall with her chin held high and her arms empty. "I'm moving back in my room. I'm big enough to sleep in there, and that makes me big enough to go to school."

Roxie rolled her eyes. "Faye, you have to be five to start school."

"I don't care! I'm going to school!" Faye walked downstairs, holding the shiny rail with one small hand. At the bottom of the steps she looked back up at Roxie. "I am going to put all my clothes in my dresser, and I am going to sleep in my room. So there!"

"Go right ahead," said Roxie. She didn't have the patience to argue with Faye.

The phone rang, and Roxie jumped. She stood in the doorway, watching Lacy run from her room to answer. Her long auburn hair was brushed all to one side and hung over her slender shoulder. One eye was made up and the other wasn't. They looked like before and after pictures.

"Hello," said Lacy breathlessly.

Roxie turned to leave, then waited just in case it was for her. Maybe the girls wouldn't stay angry at her. Or maybe Rob would call and want to play chess.

Lacy caught Roxie's eye and frowned. "It's for me," she whispered as she listened to the person on the other end.

Roxie walked to her bed and sank to the edge. Maybe she could go find Rob and talk to him. She shook her head. Chelsea had probably told him everything. Rob might not like her after this. She couldn't take a chance on having him snap at her or say something unkind.

Lacy stopped in the doorway, and her brown eyes glowed. "I got the job, Roxie! I can start tomorrow!"

"What job?"

"The one I applied for two weeks ago at Markee's Department Store. I can start tomorrow!"

"But what about our vacation?"

Lacy shrugged. "I'll worry about that later. I have to see if I have anything to wear. This is so wonderful!"

"What about Faye?" asked Roxie.

Lacy whirled around, her hand over her mouth. "I forgot all about her! Roxie, you'll take care of her, won't you? Mom only needs help with her until Grandma's out of the hospital."

Roxie shook her head. "What about Eli? Maybe he will."

"He said he's going to be working at the grocery store again since we can't leave on vacation yet. He'll take time off later."

Faye poked her head around her bedroom door. "Nobody has to watch me. I am big enough to watch myself." She disappeared back into her room.

Lacy laughed. "What a little cutie."

Faye looked back out with a scowl. "I am not a cutie. I'm going to school! So there!"

Roxie made a face at Faye, but made sure Lacy didn't see her and scold her. Lacy acted too bossy at times.

Suddenly the phone rang again. Roxie almost jumped out of her skin. She watched Lacy whiz down the hallway to the phone. She answered it and frowned, then held it out to Roxie.

"It's for you," Lacy said in surprise.

Roxie's heart stopped for an instant, then thundered on.

Lacy laid the receiver down on the tiny table and hurried back to her room.

On wooden legs Roxie walked to the phone. "Hello," she said hoarsely.

"It's Chelsea."

Roxie almost slammed down the receiver. She gripped it so tight her knuckles turned white. "What d' you want?"

"I saw the flower bed."

"So?"

"I can fix it."

Roxie wanted to agree, but instead said, "Mom gave the job to me. She said she wouldn't even pay you for what you did do."

Chelsea was quiet a long time. "I thought you wanted her to win the PRETTIEST FLOWERS CONTEST."

"I do!"

"She can't win if you don't fix the flower bed right."

"I can fix it right!"

"I just wanted to help."

"I don't need you," said Roxie stiffly. But she did! Why couldn't she tell Chelsea that?

"I didn't tell the others what you did."

Roxie sank weakly against the wall. "You didn't?"

"No."

"Why not?"

"I just didn't."

Roxie closed her eyes. "I gotta go."

"Okay. Bye."

Roxie swallowed hard. "Bye," she whispered. She hung up and slowly walked to her room, shaking her head. Why hadn't Chelsea told on her?

6

The Surprise Visitors

Roxie heard the doorbell ring, and her heart dropped to her feet. Had Chelsea decided to come see her since she'd hung up so quickly? Roxie ran to her window and looked down. She couldn't see the front door, but she did see a brown station wagon parked outside the garage. "Who is it?" she muttered.

"Answer the door, Roxie!" called Lacy impatiently.

"You get it!" shouted Roxie.

"Roxann Shoulders, answer the door right now!" cried Lacy.

Sighing heavily, Roxie walked slowly downstairs to the front door. She should've locked her bedroom door and refused to answer the door, but she knew Lacy would keep after her until she obeyed. "Lacy is too bossy," whispered Roxie for the millionth time that week. She reached the door just as the bell rang again.

She opened it and gasped in surprise. Uncle Gabe and Aunt Joylene stood there with their three children—Angel who was sixteen, Meg fifteen, and Sean thirteen. And they all had luggage! "Hi," Roxie said weakly.

"Is your mom home?" asked Uncle Gabe as he stepped inside, waited for his family to follow, then closed the door. He was Mom's brother, and he hadn't visited them in almost a year. He sometimes got mad at Grandma and stayed away.

"She's probably at the hospital," said Aunt Joylene before Roxie could say anything. "Roxie, show us where we can sleep."

Roxie looked helplessly behind her in hopes Lacy or Eli had come downstairs. They hadn't. "I don't know what to tell you," said Roxie, backing away. "Mom didn't say anything."

"She didn't know we were coming," said Uncle Gabe, rattling the change and keys in the pocket of his blue dress slacks. He had a medium build with a rounded stomach from eating too many of the things he baked in the bakery in Detroit where he worked.

"We didn't know until the last minute," said Aunt Joylene. "But we knew your parents would want us to stay here with them. We want to help keep up their spirits." She smiled, showing white teeth behind her bright red lipstick. Her blonde hair hung to her slender shoulders. She was a fourth grade teacher and often sounded like one, even to her own kids.

"I want to get settled in so I can get on over to the hospital," said Uncle Gabe. "I suspect you want us upstairs."

Roxie nodded weakly. She glanced at her cousins, but they were busy looking around the living room. Roxie remembered how much they liked watching TV or movies on the VCR.

Roxie said, "Sean, you can share Eli's room. He's in there now. I don't know how clean it'll be." Mom and Dad were always after Eli to clean his room, but even after he cleaned it, it was a mess.

Sean walked up the stairs and opened Eli's door just as the others reached the top of the steps.

"Sean!" cried Eli in shock. He poked his head out, let Sean in, said hello to the others, then quickly shut the door.

Lacy looked out her door and gasped in surprise.

Faye opened her door. "This is not the spare room now," she said crisply. "Nobody can sleep in here." She closed the door with a snap.

"She's turned into a sassy little girl, hasn't she?" said Aunt Joylene with a frown.

Roxie didn't take time to explain what was

going on with Faye. "Lacy, they're staying with us," said Roxie weakly. "Where shall we put them?"

"I don't know," said Lacy, seeming to be at a loss.

"I'll take care of it," said Aunt Joylene. She looked in Roxie's room, then in Lacy's. "Hmmm. Both have double beds. We'll sleep in here since it has a private bathroom," she said, indicating Lacy's room. "Angel and Meg, you sleep in there." She pointed to Roxie's room.

Roxie gasped as she looked helplessly at Lacy.

"What about us?" asked Lacy.

"I'm sure you can share that room with Faye." Aunt Joylene nodded toward Faye's closed door, then set her luggage in Lacy's bedroom and breathed a sigh of relief. "I'd like a shower before we go to the hospital to see your mother, Gabe."

"Go ahead," said Uncle Gabe as he set his luggage down. "Lacy, do you need anything from here before we take over?"

Lacy looked around helplessly. "I'll take a few things now and get the rest after you leave for the hospital."

"Fine," said Aunt Joylene. "I'm sure we can trust you not to go through our things."

Roxie bit back a sharp cry. How could Aunt Joylene even suggest such a thing of Lacy? Faye might not know better, but she and Lacy did!

"I wouldn't touch your things," said Lacy sharply.

"Don't get sassy with your aunt," said Uncle Gabe, shaking his finger at Lacy.

Roxie turned away, her face hot with anger. She walked into her room just as Angel pulled back the bedspread. "What're you doing?" asked Roxie.

"We want to rest awhile before we go watch TV," said Angel.

"Do you have any good videos?" asked Meg as she pushed back her dark hair.

"A few," said Roxie. She wanted to kick the girls out of her room, but she knew she couldn't. "They're in the chest beside the TV."

"Does that Indian family still live across the street?" asked Angel, looking out the window.

"Yes," said Roxie, bristling at the way Angel said, "Indian family."

"You're not friends with them, are you?" asked Meg with a frown.

Roxie shook her head. Right now she wasn't friends with anyone. She grabbed her nightclothes and her rollbag that she hadn't unpacked yet in case they could leave soon for their vacation.

In Faye's room Roxie dropped her things on the floor beside Lacy's, then stared at her sisters. "How can they take over our rooms?" she whispered.

"They didn't take my room," said Faye, giggling. She jumped up on her bed and stood in the middle of it with her arms out for balance. Her legs looked skinny sticking out of her blue shorts. Her feet were bare and her toenails still red from when Lacy had polished them two days ago.

Lacy shook her head. "I can't believe they did that! How will I ever get ready for work on time now that so many have to share the bathrooms?"

Roxie hadn't thought about sharing the bathrooms. If she couldn't get in the one in the hall, she'd always used Lacy's. "I hope they don't stay long," she said. She didn't want to share a room with Lacy and Faye. It was hard to think her secret thoughts and have her special daydreams with them in the same room.

"I guess we'll all three have to sleep in the same bed," said Lacy.

"Nope," said Faye, shaking her head. "It's my bed, and I'm sleeping in it all alone."

Roxie wanted to shake Faye, but she didn't. She knew Lacy would take care of her.

Lacy caught Faye's arm and pulled her close. "Faye, you will share your bed with us and that's final! And I don't want any back talk!"

"Okay," whispered Faye.

"It's almost time for you to eat and take your bath," said Lacy. She turned to Roxie. "We'll work together on making dinner. I guess we'll have to feed the others too."

"I'll help make dinner," said Faye. "I'm big!"

Lacy hugged Faye tight. "You can help. Let's get started."

Roxie followed them downstairs to the kitchen. She looked in the refrigerator. "It's almost empty," she said as panic rose inside her. Mom had wanted it that way because of their vacation. "What can we make?"

"Pancakes," said Faye. "I want pancakes."

Lacy laughed and hugged Faye. "I don't think the others do."

Just then Mom and Dad walked in. Mom looked pale and tired. Dad looked concerned.

"I see we have company," said Dad.

"They're upstairs," said Lacy.

Roxie leaned against the counter and listened while Lacy told what had happened.

"I can't believe they'd just walk in like that," said Mom, sounding close to tears.

"I can," said Dad grimly. "I'll go have a word with Gabe."

"Wait!" Mom caught Dad's arm. "Let them stay tonight."

"We don't have anything to feed them," said Roxie. She was surprised but glad Dad would even think about kicking Uncle Gabe out. Maybe there was more to Dad than jokes and dirty overalls.

"Don't worry about feeding them," said Dad. "They won't be eating here."

"I want pancakes," said Faye, opening the cupboard and peering inside.

"That's just what we'll have," said Mom. "Roxie, you make them. You make good pancakes."

Roxie puffed up with pride.

"Will you fix them?" asked Mom.

Roxie nodded.

Mom smiled at Roxie.

"But not for Gabe's family," said Dad firmly.

Hiding a smile at Dad's determination, Roxie pulled out the big mixing bowl as Gabe and Joylene walked into the kitchen. Roxie froze as she watched Dad's face. Would he send them away or would he back down and let them stay for dinner?

Dad waited until after he and Mom had greeted Gabe and Joylene and gave them the report on Grandma, and then he said, "We weren't expecting you and your family, Gabe, so you'll have to eat somewhere else."

"Well, I never!" cried Joylene, her face red.

"I figure you want us out of your house too," said Gabe angrily. "I might've known!"

"You can spend the night," said Mom tiredly.

"And what will we do tomorrow night and the next night?" asked Gabe.

"Don't put it on Ilene," said Dad sternly. "You could've called about staying here, but you didn't. So tomorrow you can find somewhere else to stay."

Roxie saw Uncle Gabe's anger, and she stepped close to Dad. She wanted to tell him she was proud of him, but she didn't.

Gabe glared at Ilene. "Is that how you feel?"

Roxie trembled.

"Don't ask Ilene," said Dad. "She's too upset about her mother to fight with you. But I'm not! Her fight is my fight. You're not going to take advantage of us again, Gabe."

"Now, Burt," said Joylene, smiling, "let's not get in a tiff."

Roxie waited for Dad's answer.

"I'm not in a tiff," said Dad with a laugh. "Are *you*, Joylene? Now you folks go on out to eat and give our family a chance to be together."

"It's too early for our dinner," said Joylene stiffly. "We'll just go watch TV or something."

Roxie watched them walk away, then she poured pancake mix into the bowl. Her hand shook, and she looked quickly at Mom or Dad to see if they'd noticed. They hadn't, and she was glad.

Later she sat at her place at the table and watched the family eat the large pancakes she'd made. She'd burned two, but there were enough good ones to go around. Eli ate four of them.

"Tomorrow the doctor will let us know Grandma's test results," said Mom as she reached for her cup of coffee. "It looks good so far."

"I'm glad," said Lacy.

Roxie was too. She wanted Grandma to get out of the hospital and be all right. That was even more important than going to The Flying W.

Later Roxie walked outdoors to check Mom's flowers. She found Sean sitting under the maple tree. "Sean . . ." she said in surprise. "I thought you went out to eat."

"The others went, but I didn't want to go," he said just above a whisper.

She sat down beside him. "How come? Weren't you hungry?"

He shrugged. He picked a piece of grass and stripped it with his thumbnail.

Roxie sat quietly beside him. Twice she almost spoke, but didn't. She could tell something was bothering Sean. She didn't know what to do or say.

"I bet your dad never embarrasses you," Sean said hoarsely.

Roxie flushed.

"Mine always embarrasses me," said Sean. "Especially when he tries to get something for nothing. He wanted to get here while Aunt Ilene was at the hospital so he could get us a free place to stay and free meals. He knew you kids wouldn't know what to do."

"Oh," said Roxie. She knew Dad would never do that.

Sean pulled his thin legs tight against his thin chest. "I wish we'd stayed home."

HILDA STAHL

"But Grandma will be glad to see all of you."

"I guess."

"I don't want her to have cancer," said Roxie.

"Me neither," said Sean. "Eli said your family prayed for her."

Roxie swallowed hard. "We did."

"We didn't." Sean rubbed his hands down his legs. "I tried to."

Just then Roxie heard music from Chelsea's house. She glanced that way, but couldn't see past the bush. She looked toward the flower bed, and her heart sank. It looked worse than before. Maybe she'd have to ask for Chelsea's help after all. "Sean, do you know anything about gardening?"

Sean shook his head. "Why?"

"See that?" Roxie pointed to the flower bed.

"It looks dead."

"I know. I need to fix it, and I don't know how."

"That's too bad." Sean watched a car drive past. "They'll be back soon."

Roxie looked at the street just as the brown station wagon drove into sight. She felt Sean stiffen. "Don't you like your dad at all?" asked Roxie.

"Sure I do. I love him. Most of the time he's great, but sometimes he really really embarrasses me."

Roxie sat quietly a long time. She knew just what Sean meant. She was beginning to realize that what embarrassed her about her dad was nothing compared to Sean's dad. She should be proud of Dad even if he did wear dirty overalls and act like a kid.

Just then Eli burst from the house with Dad on his heels. They were laughing hard. Dad tackled Eli, and they sprawled on the grass and wrestled. They didn't stop even when Uncle Gabe, Aunt Joylene, and the girls stopped to watch them.

Roxie blushed to the roots of her hair. "That embarrasses me," she whispered to Sean.

"I wish my dad would play with me like that," said Sean wistfully.

Roxie shot a surprised look at Sean. He was serious! She turned back to watch Dad and Eli. Slowly her embarrassment faded. She heard their laughter and saw the fun they were having.

Why, it wasn't anything to be embarrassed about! A laugh bubbled up inside her and burst out before she could stop it.

7

Good News

Roxie stepped away from the ruined flower bed, her hands on the pain in her back. The maple tree blocked out the morning sun. Faye was around back playing in the sandbox. Roxie looked at the plants and groaned. "What will I do?"

"We came to help."

Roxie spun around. Chelsea, Hannah, and Kathy stood there with boxes of plants in their hands. They were dressed in shorts and T-shirts, and all three were smiling as if she'd never done anything to hurt them.

"Those flowers are dead," said Chelsea, motioning to the plants in the flower bed.

"So we hunted around and found some plants we could buy," said Hannah.

"They're different colors and different kinds of flowers," said Kathy as she set her box down. "But they'll be beautiful together, Chelsea says!"

Roxie's eyes filled with tears. She couldn't find the strength to yell at the girls and make them leave. "Why are you doing this?" she asked weakly.

"We're your friends," said Hannah with a shrug. Her long braid slid across her back as she set her box on the grass.

"We signed a pact," said Kathy. She pushed her wide green band back further on her blonde curls.

"Best friends forever," said Chelsea as she set her box down. Her red braids bounced as she jumped back up. She laughed. "Best friends forever!"

Roxie bowed her head. Never in her life had she expected them to do such a nice thing for her! How could they think she'd been a best friend? "I've been so mean," she whispered.

"We forgive you," said Kathy, spreading her hands wide. "Jesus said to, so we did."

"Now we're ready to plant these flowers," said Chelsea as she knelt down at the flower bed.

"Tell us what to do and we'll do it, Chel," said Hannah. "You're the one with the green thumb."

"Shall I fill the watering can with water?" asked Roxie as she picked it up.

Chelsea felt the soil. "No. It's plenty wet." She pulled out plants that were already dead and put them in a pile.

She motioned to the few plants left standing. "These will be all right." She scratched around in the dirt with her small hand rake. "I'll make holes where the plants should be." She dug a hole with a small hoe, then laid it down and picked up a plant. "Here's how to plant them." She put the root of a plant into a hole, then pressed soil around it. "You can each one take one and plant it. It won't take long to finish with all of us working together."

"How's your grandma?" asked Hannah as she stuck a plant in another hole Chelsea had dug.

"We'll know today," said Roxie as she pressed soil around the flower she'd planted. She sat back on her heels and told them about her aunt and uncle. "Grandma said they could stay in her house while they're here. They didn't want to because they don't want to clean up after themselves." Roxie sighed heavily. "They might leave her house dirty."

"Then we'll clean the house after they leave!" cried Hannah with an excited laugh. "We'll ask someone to drive us there, and we'll clean it."

"And we'll do it as our good deed," said Kathy. They never took pay for a good deed.

Roxie bit her lip to hold back a sob. Clean Grandma's house? And for no pay? "How can you be nice to me after what I did?" she asked hoarsely.

"Jesus helps us," said Chelsea softly. "His love is in us." She tapped Roxie's arm. "And in you."

"It doesn't seem like it," said Roxie around the lump in her throat.

"The Bible says God's love is shed abroad in

our hearts by the Holy Spirt. And the Bible is true," said Kathy.

"But if you don't know what's in the Bible, you don't know what promises are yours," said Hannah.

"You can love like Jesus does, Roxie," said Chelsea.

"You can," said Hannah and Kathy.

Suddenly Roxie wanted that more than anything. "Then I will!" cried Roxie. She brushed at her tears. "But how do I do it?"

"Jesus will help you," said Kathy.

Roxie looked at the girls in awe. "How do you girls know so much about Jesus?"

"We read the Bible," they said together.

"I don't," said Roxie, hanging her head. Nobody had ever said she should. Or maybe they had and she hadn't listened.

"We'll help you," said Chelsea, looking over her shoulder as she knelt at the flower bed.

"We agreed to help each other," said Kathy as she wiped her hands on the grass to get the dirt off. "I'll give you a Scripture when you call me."

Roxie sat back and studied the girls in wonder. They were serious! Even though she'd been mean to them, they were helping her and they'd keep on helping her. Awesome!

Finally the girls stepped away from the flower bed. The plants all looked healthy and strong. A few had yellow flowers blooming.

"We have to cut off the blooms," said Chelsea as she picked up a pair of scissors that she'd brought just for that reason.

"Don't cut them!" cried Roxie. "They look too pretty."

Chelsea shook her head. "If I don't cut them, the plant won't develop like it should. I have to cut the flowers off to give the plant strength. Then more flowers will grow."

Roxie wanted to insist Chelsea not cut the flowers, but she knew Chelsea was right. "I won't argue with you. You really do have a green thumb!"

Chelsea laughed. "Sure do! Two of them!" She held up her dirty thumbs. "They sure look brown right now though."

"We all have brown thumbs," said Kathy, giggling.

They all laughed, washed their hands off at the outside spigot, then sat under the maple tree.

"We have new people calling for the *King's Kids*," said Chelsea. "We have several jobs lined up, but still no opening for you, Roxie. When we do, we'll let you know."

"Thanks," said Roxie.

"We're having my dad and Chelsea's dad check out the people we don't know," said Hannah. "It's not safe to work for folks we don't know."

They talked for several minutes, then the girls said they had to leave.

"Thanks for your help," said Roxie stiffly. She wished she could let them see how really thankful she was, but she felt too awkward.

"You're welcome," said Chelsea, smiling.

"Call us when you hear the news about your grandma," said Hannah.

"I will have a Scripture ready for you when you call me," said Kathy with a happy smile.

Roxie nodded as she watched the girls leave. It seemed impossible that they'd actually helped her after she'd been so unkind to them. Was it really possible for her to be nice with Jesus' help?

In the middle of the afternoon Mom and Dad walked into the kitchen, where Roxie was having graham crackers and milk with Faye. Mom looked ready to burst with excitement. Dad swept Faye up in his arms and hugged her tight, then kissed Roxie's cheek.

"Good news!" said Mom, beaming.

"What?" asked Roxie.

"Grandma doesn't have cancer!" cried Mom, brushing a tear off her cheek. "She needs to rest a few days after all the tests, so she's going to come here in the morning after she's released from the hospital."

"Hooray!" shouted Faye, sounding just like Dad.

"Here?" asked Roxie in a weak voice. She was thinking of her terrible secret.

"She'll have to sleep in our room since she is too weak to go up and down stairs," said Mom. "We'll sleep in the spare room."

Faye shook her head hard. "There is no spare room! It's my room!"

"I'd forgotten," said Mom, grinning.

Dad tugged Faye's ponytail. "You can give up your room for the few nights Grandma is here. You can sleep with Roxie."

Roxie forced back a groan. Last night had been hard enough sleeping with Faye in between her and Lacy. Faye kicked in her sleep.

"I guess I can sleep with Roxie," said Faye. "But I'm still big enough to go to school even if I don't sleep in my own bed."

Roxie rolled her eyes, but didn't say anything. She'd let Mom and Dad deal with Faye.

Later she remembered to tell Mom about the girls cleaning Grandma's house. "We'll do it for free if someone will drive us there," Roxie said.

"I'll take you myself," said Mom as she hugged Roxie. "That's very sweet and generous for you girls to take on such a job without pay. I'm sorry to say I know how Gabe and his family will leave the house."

The next morning Roxie and Faye waited on the front step for Mom and Dad to bring Grandma home. Lacy and Eli were both at work. Uncle Gabe and his family had said good-bye to Grandma at the hospital, then had gone home.

"It's such a sudden decision that we couldn't straighten up the house," Uncle Gabe had said.

"We'll take care of it," Mom had said. "Roxie and her friends will do it."

"That's good," Aunt Joylene had said. "They need something to keep them occupied. Children nowadays don't have enough responsibility."

Roxie had seen anger jump in Dad's eyes, but he'd kept quiet. She had been very proud of him.

Now as she watched for them Roxie realized she'd been proud of Dad several times in the past two days. Was Dad changing that much? Or maybe she was!

A few minutes later Dad parked the station wagon outside the garage. Grandma got out. Her gray hair was neatly combed. She wore black dress pants and a light blue blouse with tiny pink and yellow flowers on the collar. She looked the same, only a little thinner and a little tired. Roxie had thought she'd look really sick.

With Faye beside her Roxie ran to Grandma and hugged her. "I'm glad you don't have cancer," said Roxie.

"Me too," said Grandma. "God took care of me!"

Roxie hadn't heard Grandma say that before, but she was glad she did.

71

Faye hugged Grandma tight. "We don't have a spare room any more," Faye said. "So you can't sleep in it."

"That's all right," said Grandma as she kissed Faye's cheek.

In Mom and Dad's bedroom Grandma sank to the edge of the bed. "I'm going to take a little nap right now, but I'll be up for lunch," she said.

"Are you sure you want to sleep in here all alone?" asked Faye. "Sleeping alone is scary sometimes." She opened her eyes wide. "But not to big girls like me!"

"I'll be just fine," said Grandma. She looked thoughtfully at Roxie. "You know, it might be better if someone slept on the cot in here just in case I need a hand during the night."

Roxie stiffened. Grandma couldn't mean her!

"Roxann, will you sleep in here with me?" asked Grandma softly.

"Of course she will!" said Mom, nodding. "That's a fine idea. And we'll sleep in your room, Roxie. Faye can have her room to herself."

"Oh," said Faye in a tiny voice.

Roxie wanted to refuse, but she nodded. Maybe Grandma wouldn't say anything about the phone call. If she did, she could say she'd written the number down, but had forgotten to give it to Mom. Roxie's stomach knotted painfully.

"Let's let Grandma rest," said Dad, herding

them out the door. "Do you need anything before you lie down?"

"No," said Grandma as she slipped off her black flats. She had short, stubby toes just like Roxie's.

Roxie turned away from the short, stubby toes and followed Faye out of the bedroom.

A few minutes later Roxie called Chelsea, Hannah, then Kathy to tell them the good news about Grandma. She called Kathy last so she would receive a Scripture. What if Kathy forgot?

Just as Roxie was saying good-bye, Kathy said, "Here's the Scripture for you. Be sure to write it down so you can look it up in your Bible."

Roxie pulled the pad and pencil out of the tiny drawer. It made her think of Grandma's call, and she trembled.

"Ready?" asked Kathy.

"Yes," said Roxie.

"It's James chapter 4 and verse 7."

Roxie wrote it down.

"It says, 'Submit to God. Resist the devil and he will flee from you.'"

Roxie frowned.

"It means to do what God wants you to do. When you're tempted to do wrong, say no to the devil and he will run away fast. He always tries to get us to do wrong. But if we submit to God and resist the devil, we won't do wrong."

Roxie leaned weakly against the wall. It sounded so easy. Would she be able to submit to God and resist the devil? She said good-bye, then slowly walked to her bedroom. She picked up her Bible, hunted until she found James 4:7, then read it aloud.

"I will do what God wants!" she said with a firm shake of her head.

At bedtime Roxie laid on the cot across the room from Grandma's bed. "Good night, Grandma," Roxie said softly.

"Good night, Roxann."

Roxie stared up at the ceiling. The room was darker than hers, but she could still see shadows and outlines. It smelled different than her room too. Hers smelled like apple-and-spice potpourri—her favorite smell. This room smelled like Grandma's dusting powder that she'd used after her shower.

"Roxann, I must ask you something," said Grandma.

Roxie froze. "What?" she asked with a catch in her voice.

"About the phone call the day I went in the hospital. I know you didn't tell your mother. That made me feel sad. Why didn't you tell her?"

Roxie started to say she'd written down the number, but forgot to tell her mom in the excitement of leaving on vacation. Then she remembered James 4:7. She knew God didn't want her to lie, but the devil did. She said the Scripture over in her head three times. Finally she said, "I'm sorry, Grandma. I didn't want to tell Mom because I thought we'd get a late start on our vacation."

"I thought as much," said Grandma.

"I'm sorry," said Roxie. And she meant it!

"I'm glad you told the truth," said Grandma. "Never never lie, Roxann."

"I won't," she vowed. But was it possible to keep her promise? She thought of James 4:7, smiled, and nodded in the dark.

8

The Only Job

Roxie dried off the kitchen table, set the basket of wooden fruit back in place, then hung up the dishtowel. She thought of the long day stretching out in front of her. She didn't have to watch Faye since Mom was home. Roxie glanced up as Mom walked back into the kitchen after seeing if Grandma wanted anything else.

"I'll drive you girls to Grandma's house this afternoon," said Mom.

"Thanks."

Mom filled her cup with coffee, poured in a little milk, and sipped the coffee. "With four of you working it shouldn't take you more than an hour."

"We'll do a good job."

"I'm sure you will." Mom sighed heavily. "I hate to see my own brother act the way he does. It's embarrassing, and it hurts."

Roxie raised her brows in surprise. She'd never thought about Mom getting embarrassed!

"He has a lot of potential. I sometimes think he's frustrated because he's not doing something with his art. Sure, he decorates cakes and he bakes fancy things, but it's not the same."

"I didn't know he had talent in art," said Roxie. She thought of her own talent that she wasn't using.

"He's a better artist than I am," said Mom. "I know I do a good job on the little animals I carve and the watercolors I paint. Gabe could make the same things I do, and they'd have that special something that makes art great. His work touches hearts. Mine is good enough to sell, but it's nothing like his."

Roxie leaned back against the counter. Mom had never talked to her like this before—like she was an adult. It felt good.

"Gabe has the same talent Grandpa had."

"I didn't know that." Roxie felt the same longing for Grandpa that she always felt when she thought about him. He'd died last year, and it still seemed funny that he wasn't around to talk to her. She missed him a lot, and so did her family. But Grandma missed him the most. Roxie knew he was in Heaven and that he was happy, but she wanted him back, and so did Grandma.

"Some talented people are afraid to do their

art, in case nobody likes it. Gabe's that way." Mom studied Roxie for a while. "And so are you, Roxie."

She flushed painfully. "But my work isn't that good!"

"It's good for your age, Roxie. If you keep being creative, you'll get better. You'll find the medium that suits you best. It might be doing crafts or it might be painting with oils or watercolors or acrylics. That mouse you carved was very well done."

"Some kids at school laughed at it."

"So what? No matter how good you are, there will always be someone who doesn't like your work or who laughs at you. Some people laugh just to keep you from succeeding. It makes some folks mad to see talent put to use."

Roxie hadn't thought of that. She liked carving animals, especially baby animals. She'd started by carving soap, then she'd gone to soft wood, and now she could carve almost anything. Mom let her use her tools as long as she was careful. Carving tools were very sharp. So far she hadn't cut herself once. But then, she hadn't carved in several months—not since Jason Woods had laughed at her mouse.

Mom sat at the table with her coffee. "Roxie, don't let what other people think or say stop you from doing what is right. You get embarrassed too easily over things."

Roxie nodded as she flushed painfully. She hadn't thought Mom had noticed.

"If I let others rule me, I'd be working at a regular job away from home, and someone else would be raising you children." Mom leaned back and looked off into space. "It's hard for women to stay home instead of going out into the work force. It'll be even worse when you grow up." She looked right at Roxie. "Don't let anyone tell you you must get a job or you're not worthwhile. A woman is worthwhile when she stays home with her kids. When you get married and you have kids, if you want to stay home with them, do it. You'll still be valuable and happy."

Roxie nodded but only because she liked having Mom talk to her—the future seemed too far away to think about. It never occurred to her that she'd have to decide whether to get a job or stay home when she got older. Right now it felt like she'd be twelve years old all her life.

Mom pushed back her gray-streaked brown hair. "I don't think I've told you, Roxie, but I'm very proud of the way you've been helping with Faye and making money by working."

The words warmed Roxie's heart. "Thanks."

"When's your next job?"

"I don't know." Roxie told Mom about the jobs being taken because of their vacation plans.

"Something will turn up," said Mom. "Go call

the girls and set up a time for this afternoon to clean Grandma's house. I still can't get over how nice it is for you to do it without pay. That's very sweet of all of you."

Roxie grinned and shrugged. She wasn't used to Mom praising her so much. "I'll call Chelsea," she said as she walked away. Chelsea would know the free time for the others.

Roxie used the phone in the hallway upstairs. Chelsea answered on the third ring.

"Roxie, I was just ready to call you," said Chelsea.

"Oh? Why?"

"I have a job for you." Chelsea paused. "If you want it."

Roxie frowned. Why did Chelsea sound so funny? "Why wouldn't I want it?"

"It's working for . . . for Ezra Menski."

Roxie gripped the receiver tightly. She didn't want to work for him or to have to see his dog Gracie. "Is it the only job?"

"Yes."

Roxie slid down the wall and sat on the carpet. "What does he need done?"

"His dishes."

"His dishes!" Roxie shook her head. How she hated doing dishes!

"'Great or small, we do it all,'" Chelsea quoted from their business flyer.

"But dishes!"

"He said he let them pile up and he can't get to them. He said his hands have been hurting him."

Roxie was quiet a long time. She twisted the cord around her finger. Downstairs she heard Faye singing. "Are you sure it's the only job?"

"Yes," said Chelsea, sounding sorry that it was.

"Oh, all right! I'll take it." Was she really serious? She nodded to herself. She was desperate. Doing nothing was really boring. "When does he want me?"

"ASAP."

Roxie knew that meant "as soon as possible." The first time Chelsea had said ASAP Roxie couldn't imagine what she meant. "I can be there in a few minutes."

"Good. I'll let Kathy know so she can write you down."

"Thanks." Roxie slowly stood. "Mom said she'd take us to Grandma's this afternoon to clean her house. What time should I tell her we can do it?"

"Three o'clock would work for us," said Chelsea. "We'll all be done with our jobs by then."

"Unless Ezra Menski has a whole kitchen full of dirty dishes," said Roxie, wrinkling her nose.

Several minutes later Roxie stood outside Ezra Menski's door. The porch was swept clean except for a tattered bedroom slipper under the rocker. Taking a deep breath, Roxie knocked. She wanted to turn and run. Ezra Menski had yelled at her many times already for chasing Gracie. Roxie shivered. She hated coming to work for him.

Ezra opened the door with a jerk, then leaned heavily on his cane as he glared at Roxie. The knuckles of his hand looked extra-large. The white hair above his ears stood on end. Gracie slipped around his legs and sniffed Roxie. She wanted to slap the little animal.

"Why're you here?" snapped Ezra, scowling down at Roxie.

She swallowed hard. "I came to do your dishes. I'm the worker the *King's Kids* sent over."

Ezra hiked up his baggy pants and shook his head. "I don't want you here."

"I thought you needed dishes washed," said Roxie stiffly.

"I do. But I don't want the likes of you around. You hate Gracie."

Gracie barked a sharp bark, then settled at Ezra's feet.

Roxie lifted her chin and squared her shoulders. Butterflies fluttered in her stomach, but she didn't let them show. "I don't hate Gracie. I just don't like her to tear up Mom's flower bed."

"Gracie never does anything bad!"

"She tore up our flower bed!"

"It was another dog, not Gracie." Ezra rapped his cane hard on the floor. "It was not Gracie!"

"Then it was a dog that looked just like her," said Roxie, struggling hard to keep her temper.

Ezra rubbed his large hand over his bald head. "You might as well come in and get the dishes started. But I'll be checking on you to make sure you don't lollygag around."

Roxie walked through the clean hallway after Ezra and Gracie. She peeked in open doorways and was surprised to see the house was very clean and tidy. She stopped in the kitchen and gasped as she looked at the mess. Dirty dishes were piled on the sink, the counters, and even the round kitchen table. She wanted to run away as fast as she could.

"It's probably too hard a job for you," snapped Ezra. "You youngsters are all alike—lazy!"

She stiffened her backbone. "I'll do the dishes."

"And you'll do them *right*." Ezra thumped his cane on the blue-and-white linoleum floor. "If you leave even one dish dirty, I won't pay you."

Roxie pressed her lips tightly together. She would not fight with him! She filled the sink with hot soapy water. Then a thought occurred to her. "Do you have a dishwasher?" she asked, looking over her shoulder at Ezra.

"Yes." He rubbed his shallow cheek. "But I don't know how to use it."

Roxie looked at the cupboard beside the sink and saw the dishwasher in the same spot as in her house. It was even the exact model as theirs. "I know how to use it. Do you have soap for it?"

"Look under the sink," he snapped.

She looked under the sink and found an unopened box of dishwasher detergent. "You do," she said, lifting it out.

"Go ahead and use the dishwasher," he said gruffly. "And show me how. I might as well save myself some money after this. I can't be hiring someone to do my dishes all the time."

Roxie patiently showed Ezra how to load and start the dishwasher.

"That's not so hard," he said, shaking his head. "I don't know why I couldn't figure it out myself."

"Mom had to show me how," said Roxie.

"Yes . . . Well, I'm not a child."

Even after loading the dishwasher there were still a lot of dishes to do. "I'll wash pots and pans while it's working," she said. "Then I'll unload the dishwasher and start another load. By then all the dishes should be done."

"You can sweep and scrub the kitchen floor too," said Ezra as he walked toward the back door. "I'll be out back with Gracie."

Roxie sighed heavily as she washed and rinsed pots and pans. Finally she piled all the dirty dishes on the counter. She knew they'd all go in the next load of the dishwasher. She found the broom and swept the floor. It was really dirty. She mopped it with a sponge mop, then stood back and admired her work.

Just then the back door opened and Gracie ran in—right across the newly mopped floor, leaving black paw prints.

"Get out of here!" cried Roxie, shaking her fist at Gracie. "Look what you did!"

Ezra thumped his cane. "Don't yell at Gracie! She didn't do anything wrong."

"Just look at the floor!" Roxie waved at the paw prints. "Gracie is the only one with paws!"

Ezra nodded. "Point well taken. You'll just have to mop the floor again."

Roxie clenched her fists at her sides. How she wanted to refuse! But she didn't. She slowly nodded.

"Come, Gracie," called Ezra. "I'll take her for a walk until the floor is dry."

"Thank you," said Roxie stiffly.

She waited until they walked out. "I hope they stay away until I'm all done," she muttered. She unloaded the dishwasher, then loaded and started it again. She mopped the floor, then sank to a chair she'd set in the hallway and waited for the floor to dry. She didn't want anything to mess up her work. She dabbed sweat off her face and closed her eyes.

Later she looked around the kitchen to see if it was totally clean. She saw a counter she'd forgotten to wash, so she washed it. She moved a canister to wash under it and found a folded hundred dollar bill. "Oh my," she whispered as she fingered the money. She could take it and he'd never know. Just then she remembered her Bible verse: "Submit to God. Resist the devil and he'll flee from you." She knew stealing was a sin. "I won't steal," she said. "Thank You, Jesus, for helping me do what's right." She chuckled as she put the money right back where she'd found it. This time it was easy to do the right thing. It had even been easy to pray!

Later she stepped to the doorway and looked all around the spotless kitchen. All the dishes were put away. If they were in the wrong place, Ezra Menski would just have to look for them! The counters and stove and table were clean. She could almost see herself in the shiny floor. "I did a good job," she said proudly.

"I'll be the judge of that," said Ezra from behind her.

She jumped in surprise.

Gracie ran into the kitchen and sniffed every corner.

Scowling, Ezra looked in the cupboards. He narrowed his brown eyes as he looked at Roxie. "I guess it'll pass."

Gracie barked as if she agreed.

Ezra pulled five dollars from his baggy pants pockets. "Here. I won't need you again."

Roxie was glad to hear that. She pushed the

money in her pocket. "Thank you," she said as kindly as she could.

"And don't blame Gracie for tearing up your flower bed," snapped Ezra. "She doesn't do that."

Roxie shrugged but didn't argue. She'd learned by watching Dad with Uncle Gabe that sometimes it's better to keep quiet even if you're right.

At the front door Ezra said, "Just what is this *King's Kid* stuff all about?"

"It's ten kids doing odd jobs for people," she said.

"And who's the King?" asked Ezra.

Roxie's mouth turned bone-dry. She knew the others wouldn't have a problem saying it was Jesus, but she couldn't force out the name. She shrugged.

"You don't even know who the King is?" asked Ezra with a scowl.

"I got to get home," she said in a rush. Before Ezra Menski could say anything else, she ran down the sidewalk toward home.

Why couldn't she tell him Jesus was the King? A band tightened around her heart. Was she too embarrassed to? She bit her bottom lip. Was she as embarrassed of Jesus as she was of Dad? The terrible thought brought tears to her eyes. What was wrong with her anyway? She was probably the only person alive who was embarrassed to even say the name Jesus aloud to another person.

9

Grandma's House

Roxie knelt beside Grandma where she sat in the rocking chair in the living room. She smelled like rose perfume. Today she'd dressed in slacks and a blouse instead of staying in her housecoat. "Mom said you wanted to see me."

Grandma held Roxie's hand to her soft cheek. "I know it's hard on you to go to my house without Grandpa there, but I appreciate you going."

Roxie swallowed the lump in her throat.

"Since you are going, I'd like you to bring back a couple of things for me," said Grandma as she released Roxie's hand.

"What things?" asked Roxie.

Grandma bit her lip and dabbed at her brown eyes with the corner of her tissue. "You know the photo of Grandpa on the fireplace mantel in the living room?"

Roxie's heart jerked. "Yes."

"Bring that," whispered Grandma.

Roxie wanted to refuse, but she nodded. She hated to look at that photo. Grandpa looked so alive!

"I'd ask your mother, but she's afraid I'm still living in the past. I know you understand."

Roxie nodded. She did understand. Grandma still missed Grandpa more than she'd admit to anyone.

"And bring Grandpa's carving tools."

Roxie frowned slightly.

"Roxann, he wanted you to have them, but I couldn't part with them. Now I can. We both want you to have them."

Roxie shook her head and struggled hard not to burst into tears. Grandpa had treasured his tools. They were a craftsman's tools. She didn't deserve them. She was a long way from being a craftsman! "I . . . I can't take them, Grandma."

"You must, Roxann. Grandpa wanted you to. He said you have talent, and he wanted you to develop that talent."

"But what if I don't use them?"

"You will," said Grandma softly as she patted Roxie's hand.

Roxie wanted to argue, but she didn't. Maybe someday when she was really old she would use the tools and carve something great. "Where are the tools?" asked Roxie with a small sigh.

"In a wooden box in the bottom drawer of the tall chest of drawers in my bedroom." Grandma caught Roxie's hand again. "Roxann, thank you! I know it'll be hard for you to do what I have asked, but please do it. God is with you."

Roxie kissed Grandma's soft cheek.

A little later Roxie stepped inside Grandma's house and stood at the side of the door while the others walked in. The house smelled closed in and felt hot. Roxie blinked hard to hold back tears. She'd tried to stay away as much as possible since Grandpa had died.

Mom looked around the living room. "It's not as messy as I thought it would be. Probably the bedrooms and bathrooms are the worst." She slipped an arm around Roxie's slender shoulders. "Open the windows to air out the place. I'll be back in an hour. If you get done sooner, give me a call. Or if you see it'll take longer, call me."

Roxie nodded. She was afraid her voice would crack if she talked.

After Mom left, the house seemed very quiet. Roxie couldn't look at the fireplace and the photo. She'd get it just before they left.

"This is a nice house," said Chelsea as she walked into the kitchen. She opened the three kitchen windows, and a pleasant breeze blew in. "Probably the best thing to do is divide the rooms equally. How many rooms are there, Roxie?"

"Three bedrooms, two bathrooms, kitchen, dining room, living room, laundry room, and a basement," said Roxie as she leaned against an arrowback oak kitchen chair. Grandma had told her the oak table and chairs had been her great-grandmother's. Someday it would go to Lacy. Lacy didn't like to talk about that because it meant Grandma would be dead.

"Roxie, you choose what you want to clean," said Chelsea. "We know it's hard on you to be here."

Roxie gasped in surprise. "How did you know?"

"By your face," said Chelsea.

Roxie flushed to the roots of her dark hair. She couldn't get used to anyone noticing how she felt, or caring about how she felt for that matter. "I'll take Grandma's bedroom." She hesitated. "And the living room."

"My great-grandpa died in January," said Hannah. "It was very sad for us, but happy for him."

"Because he went to be with Jesus, right?" said Kathy.

Hannah nodded.

"I'm scared to die," said Roxie just above a whisper. She had never admitted that to anyone in her entire life.

"Granddad said it was just leaving earth and

going to live at a new place," said Hannah. She patted her chest as she went on, "Our bodies are just our earth suits. When it's time for our spirits to go be with the Lord, our bodies stop working and our spirits live on."

"But if you don't know Jesus as your personal Savior your spirit goes to Hell," said Kathy. "That's what the Bible says."

"Granddad knew Jesus," said Hannah.

"So did my grandpa," said Roxie. She remembered the time five years ago when Grandpa had told the family about accepting Jesus as his Savior. They were all surprised.

"Then he lives in Heaven," said Chelsea. "He moved away from Middle Lake, Michigan, and he moved to Heaven."

Roxie hadn't thought of it that way. It made her feel better. "This boy at school told me when you're dead you're dead," Roxie said, moving from one foot to the next.

"He doesn't know what the Bible says," said Kathy. "Next time you see him, tell him the truth."

Roxie turned quickly away. She could never do that! She wasn't brave enough.

"We'd better get to work," said Chelsea after she assigned everyone the rooms they were to take. She had assigned herself the kitchen and the dining room. There were dirty dishes in the sink and something sticky on the floor.

Roxie walked slowly to Grandma's bedroom. The queen-size bed looked large in the room. The tall chest stood between two windows, and a wide dresser with a huge mirror stood against the wall with the walk-in closet. The light was still on in the closet. The bed was messed up, and two dresser drawers hung open. Roxie was glad Grandma hadn't seen the room this way. She'd know Uncle Gabe and his family had snooped. Grandma hated for people to look through her personal things.

Roxie quickly opened the windows, then changed the sheets. Mom had said to bundle up the dirty linen to take back home to launder. When the room was finished Roxie stood in front of the tall chest and looked at the bottom drawer. She didn't want to open it and take out Grandpa's special tools. She didn't want them in her room to remind her of Grandpa or her special talent.

She bent down and opened the drawer. Oh, she could not look inside! She took a deep breath and finally looked. It wasn't possible! The drawer had nothing in it! "Empty!" she cried, dropping to her knees to get a better look. It was indeed empty!

"What's wrong, Roxie?" asked Hannah, running into the bedroom.

"I can't believe it!" Roxie leaped up, her cheeks flushed bright red. "Grandpa's special tools are gone!"

"Girls!" called Hannah. "Come here!"

Kathy and Chelsea ran into the bedroom. "What's wrong?" they asked at the same time.

"Tell us, Roxie," said Hannah.

Roxie told the whole story about Grandpa and his tools and how he'd wanted them to be hers because of her special talent. "Grandma asked me to take them to her today so she could give them to me," said Roxie, close to tears. "What will Grandma say if I can't find the tools?"

"This doesn't look good," said Chelsea.

"Before we panic and jump to the wrong conclusions, let's search the house to see if the toolbox is somewhere else," said Kathy.

"Good idea," they agreed.

"We'll all search this room first, then move to the next and the next," said Chelsea. She was always very organized.

"Don't make a mess while you search," said Roxie.

Silently they looked all through the room, the closet, and the connecting bathroom. Next they looked in the bathroom in the hallway, then the other bedrooms and on to the kitchen and other rooms. They searched the basement and garage last. Neither the toolbox nor the tools were in the house.

"Someone took them," said Hannah with a firm nod. "Who would it have been?"

"My uncle Gabe," said Roxie, hanging her

head. She hated to admit her relative would do such a thing.

"Call him and ask him about it," said Chelsea.

Roxie shook her head hard.

"I'll call!" said Kathy, marching to the phone in the living room.

"Wait!" cried Roxie. "I just thought of something." She quickly told them about Sean and how his dad embarrassed him when he did terrible things. "I'll call Sean and ask him. I think he'll tell me the truth."

"Good idea," said the girls, standing aside so Roxie could get to the phone.

Roxie found the number written inside the phone book in Grandma's neat handwriting. Roxie trembled as she dialed. Aunt Joylene answered, and Roxie's tongue clung to the roof of her mouth.

"Who is this?" asked Aunt Joylene sharply.

Roxie swallowed hard. "It's Roxie. I called to talk to Sean. Is he there please?"

"How's Grandma?" asked Aunt Joylene.

"She's fine," said Roxie.

"I'm sorry we couldn't stay until she was able to go home, but we had to get back. I'm sure you know how it is."

"Yes," said Roxie. "May I speak to Sean?"

"Of course." Joylene called, "Sean, Roxie's on the phone. She wants to talk to you."

Roxie waited only a few seconds before Sean said, "Hi."

Roxie heard Aunt Joylene on the extension. "Sean, how are you?" asked Roxie while she searched her brain for a way to get her aunt off the phone.

"I got it, Mom," Sean said. The receiver clicked, and Sean said, "We can talk now."

"I hate to ask you this, Sean, but I need to know." Roxie looked at the girls for support, and they all silently encouraged her to speak.

"What is it?" asked Sean.

"Did your dad or someone in your family take Grandpa's special carving tools?" Her stomach knotted as she waited for an answer.

"Why do you ask?" Sean said weakly.

"Grandma asked me to get them for her, and they're gone."

Sean sighed heavily. "Dad took the toolbox. He said he knew Grandpa wanted him to have it. But I found a note inside the box to you from Grandpa. He wanted *you* to have it. But Dad wouldn't listen to me."

"A note for me?"

"Yes."

"Oh my," whispered Roxie.

"I'll send it to you. I kept it when Dad said to throw it away."

"Thanks, Sean."

"I'm sorry Dad took the tools."

"I hate to tell Grandma. She'll feel terrible."

"I know."

Silently Roxie prayed, *Jesus, help me know what to do.* The prayer surprised her. She hadn't known she was going to do it. But she was glad she had. Jesus would help her. Finally she said, "Sean, I'll tell Dad what happened. He'll know what to do." Had she really said that? But she knew she believed it. Dad *would* know what to do.

"I'm sorry," Sean said again.

"I know," Roxie said. "It's not your fault."

"I know, but I still feel terrible."

She desperately wanted to tell him Jesus would help him, but she couldn't get the words out. "Bye, Sean. Thanks for your help."

Roxie hung up and told the girls what had happened. "Dad will take care of it. Let's finish cleaning before my mom gets here."

The girls left the living room, and Roxie walked to the fireplace. She lifted down the photo of Grandpa. He was standing beside a table of his carvings of wild birds native to Michigan. He looked proud and happy. "I know you're in Heaven, Grandpa," she whispered. "I'll try to remind Grandma so she won't feel so sad." Roxie set the photo beside the phone where she could pick it up as she left.

Suddenly the phone rang. She jumped back, grinned sheepishly, then answered it.

"Roxie, I'm sorry, but I can't come get you." It was Mom. "I asked Lacy to stop on her way home from work. If you girls get done, watch TV or something."

"We'll be all right, Mom." A chill ran down Roxie's spine. "Is something wrong?"

"No . . . Well, yes . . . It's Faye. I think she walked to the school by herself. You know how determined she is to go."

Roxie flushed painfully. Just this morning she'd told Faye she couldn't go to school because she was too young to find her way. She should've known that Faye would be determined to prove her wrong. "Mom, she'll probably take the long way past the park. That's the way she and I walked together a few days ago."

"Thanks, Roxie. I know she'll be all right, but she's so little!"

"She thinks she's big, Mom."

"I know," Mom said, sounding tired.

"Mom, I'm closer to the school than you are. I'll run over there and see if she's there."

"Have one of the girls go with you," Mom said. "I'll drive the route you said. If you find her, stay at the school and I'll pick her up."

Roxie hung up and called the girls. She told

them what had happened. Chelsea said she'd go with Roxie.

"If Lacy gets here before we get back, have her wait," said Roxie.

"We will," said Kathy. "Chel, I'll finish your work."

"Thanks," said Chelsea.

"I'll do yours," said Hannah to Roxie.

She smiled her thanks, and she and Chelsea ran out of the house and raced toward the school two blocks away. The kids from The Ravines rode a bus to school, and the ones living on this side of town walked. There was only one elementary school in Middle Lake. Roxie had attended it before she graduated into Middle School.

In the middle of the block ahead Roxie saw the large brick school building with the huge play area. She saw Faye huddled against the front door.

"I'll wait here," Chelsea said, stopping on the sidewalk that led up to the door.

"Thanks," Roxie said. She slowed to a walk, then bent down to Faye. "Hi."

Faye looked up, her ashen face wet with tears. "I got scared, Roxie. Nobody was here, and I got scared."

"You shouldn't have walked all the way by yourself, Faye. I would've walked with you."

"You said I couldn't go to school if I couldn't even find my way. I found my way."

"I know you did. But don't ever do it again. Even I don't walk this far alone. See?" Roxie pointed to Chelsea. "She came with me. It's not safe to walk alone even if you're big."

"I want to go home," whispered Faye as she rubbed her eyes with her fingertips.

"Mom is coming to pick you up. She'll be here soon."

"She'll be mad."

"I know. But it's because she was afraid for you."

"I want to go to school," Faye said with a sob.

"You have to be five," Roxie said as patiently as she could. "You can go next year."

"No! No! I want to go now!"

Just then Mom stopped the car with a screech of brakes and ran to Faye. "I'm so glad I found you!" She held Faye close and said over her head, "Thanks, Roxie."

Roxie nodded and smiled. "We'll go back to Grandma's and finish cleaning."

Mom agreed as she walked Faye to the car.

As they drove away Chelsea said, "Faye could go to preschool. They have one at the church I go to."

Roxie had gone to the Sunday school picnic, and she remembered how many kids were there. "That's a good idea, Chelsea. I'll tell Mom and Dad. It would sure make Faye happy."

"She probably gets lonely being home alone all day long while the rest of you are in school. I remember Mike used to."

"I hated to start school," Roxie said. "I cried every day for a long, long time." Suddenly she realized she'd never told anyone that before. It felt good to tell it to Chelsea. Was it possible they were really beginning to be best friends?

10

A Talk with Dad

Roxie walked through Grandma's house with the girls. "It looks great," she said with pride. The smells of furniture polish and bathroom cleaner hung in the air. "Thanks for helping."

"We were glad to," said Chelsea, and the others agreed.

In the living room Roxie picked up Grandpa's photo. "Grandma wants me to take this to her. She really misses him."

"I think we should help your grandma find something exciting to do," said Kathy. "It'll help her be happy even with your grandpa gone."

While they waited for Lacy, the girls sat in Grandma's living room and discussed things for her to do. Before long they started getting silly and said all kinds of ridiculous things that *nobody's* grandma would do. Roxie giggled as hard as the others at the idea of her grandma becoming a sky diver or climbing Mount Rainier way out in Washington State. It felt good to sit in Grandma's house and giggle after being sad in it for so long.

The door opened, and Lacy walked in. She frowned at Roxie. "What're you giggling about?"

The giggle died in Roxie's throat. "We were making plans for Grandma so she'd be happy again."

Lacy cleared her throat and looked nervous. "Let's go."

The girls jumped up. Roxie picked up the photo, while Chelsea and Hannah grabbed the bundles of dirty sheets.

"Put that picture back right now, Roxie!" snapped Lacy, shaking her car keys at the picture.

Roxie shook her head. "Grandma said to take it to her."

Lacy shivered. "Oh, all right! Just turn it so I can't see it."

Roxie knew how Lacy was feeling, but she didn't know what to say to make her feel better.

Chelsea said, "Your grandpa's living in Heaven now, Lacy. He's with Jesus."

Lacy flushed and looked uncomfortable. Roxie noticed, but the girls didn't. All the way home they talked about earth suits, moving to Heaven, and being happy with Jesus. Roxie watched out the window with Grandpa's picture pressed to her chest.

She couldn't join in the conversation, and she couldn't look to see how Lacy was taking it.

Lacy parked outside their garage, and the girls scrambled from the car, saying "Thank you" noisily.

"You're a good driver," said Kathy, smiling at Lacy. "I can't wait until I can get my driver's license."

Roxie started toward the house, then stopped short. Ezra Menski stood at the front door! He was talking to Grandma! He seemed very tall, and she seemed very short. "Why is *he* here?" muttered Roxie with a shiver. He hadn't seen her. She swerved to head for the back door before he spotted her.

"Roxann, come here," called Grandma.

Roxie's heart sank, but she walked to the front door and even managed a small smile. For once Gracie wasn't with Ezra. Maybe she was off tearing up someone else's flowers. "Hello," Roxie said weakly.

"Roxann, Ezra can't find a blue earthenware mug of his. Do you remember where you put it?"

Roxie frowned thoughtfully as she tried to remember. She glanced up and froze at the look in Ezra's piercing brown eyes. It shattered every thought in her head. "I can't remember," she said hoarsely.

"You broke it!" snapped Ezra. "You broke it and you threw it away so I wouldn't notice!"

Helplessly Roxie shook her head.

"You're scaring the child," said Grandma sharply. "Both of you calm down now. Roxann, think carefully."

She tried, but she couldn't remember seeing a blue mug. "I know I didn't break it," she said.

"Likely story!" Ezra thumped his cane on the step.

"I'll find it for you!" cried Roxie, turning away. "I'll go right now and look and I'll find it."

"Wait, Roxann," said Grandma. "The picture."

Roxie suddenly remembered the photo in her hands. She thrust it at Grandma but dropped it. They both reached for it, but Ezra caught it before it hit the steps.

"Who's this?" he asked as he looked at it.

"My late husband," said Grandma with a catch in her voice.

"Nice picture." Ezra held it out to Grandma. "I like the birds."

"He carved them," said Grandma proudly.

"That's remarkable!"

"His name was Mason Potter. You might've heard of him."

Ezra rubbed a hand over his balding head. "Mason Potter! Of course I've heard of him. I've studied his work. I carve too."

"You do?" asked Grandma, sounding interested.

Roxie moved from one foot to the other. She knew they'd forgotten about her. She wanted to leave, but if she tried they'd call her back, so she waited while they talked about carving birds and animals and masks and American Indians.

"I have a small brown beagle Mason Potter carved," said Ezra. "Looks like Gracie, so I just had to have it."

"I'd like to see it sometime," said Grandma with tears glistening in her eyes. "It's not often I get to see his work once it's been sold."

"You're welcome to come see it now," said Ezra.

Grandma shook her head. "I really can't. I'm recuperating and don't have the strength today. But I will one of these days. I promise you that."

"I could bring it over," said Ezra, smiling.

Roxie couldn't believe the change in Ezra's looks when he smiled. He didn't seem to be the same person. Maybe he wasn't so bad after all. Grandma seemed to like him.

"That would be fine. I'd better go rest now," said Grandma, holding the photo close to her heart. "Come see me when you return, Roxann."

"Yes, Grandma." Roxie's heart sank. She didn't want to tell Grandma about the missing tools.

"Your grandma seems to trust you," Ezra said as they walked away from the house.

"She does," said Roxie. She glanced back at the flower bed. Would anyone trust her if they knew what she'd done? If it hadn't been for the girls, she'd be in deep trouble.

Ezra thumped his cane. "Stop lollygagging!"

"Sorry," Roxie mumbled as her ears and neck turned red.

At Ezra's house they walked right into the kitchen. "Now, get that mug for me."

Roxie looked through each cupboard, but she couldn't find a blue earthenware mug. Chills ran down her spine. Had she broken it and forgotten? No! It had to be there somewhere!

"That's a very special mug," said Ezra gruffly. "You'd better find it!"

"I'll look again," said Roxie weakly. Maybe she'd been too upset to see clearly. She looked again, but still didn't find it. She remembered how she and the girls had looked for Grandpa's tools. Maybe she should do the same. She wished they were there to help her. She knew if she called, they'd come.

"My granddaughter made that mug for me," said Ezra gruffly. "I want it found! Unless you did break it and won't admit to it."

"I didn't," she said, but she didn't sound very convincing even to herself. "I'll look around the house. Maybe you put it down somewhere and forgot."

"Never!"

"Can I look anyway?"

He scowled so hard his eyebrows almost met over his large nose. "You think I want you snooping around my house?"

"I wouldn't snoop! I'd just look."

"I'd call it snooping!" Ezra grabbed Chelsea's ad from off the top of the refrigerator. He shook it at Roxie. "I demand my money back! It says *King's Kids* do money-back guarantee work. Give back my five dollars!"

Roxie's temper flared. "I will not! I did a good job, and I won't return your money!"

"I'll call this Chelsea McCrea girl, and I'll tell her you should be taken off the list of workers." Ezra stamped his cane hard on the kitchen floor. "Now get out of my house!"

Roxie blinked back tears as she ran from the house. When she was sure she was out of sight she let the tears flow. She ran smack into Dad.

"Hey, what's wrong?" he asked, holding her tight.

He had on his old overalls and his ugly cap, but this time she didn't care. She lifted her tear-stained face to him. "Ezra Menski thinks I broke a mug. He wants his money back for the work I did, and he wants me taken off the *King's Kid* list."

"Let's go sit down in the shade and talk about this," said Dad as he wiped away her tears with his thumbs.

She ducked her head and turned away from him. Suddenly she realized he had seen her cry! Oh, what a big baby she was! "It doesn't matter," she whispered.

"It matters," said Dad firmly. He took her arm and walked her to the big maple, then sat under the tree with her. Music floated from across the street. A dog barked in the distance.

"You didn't break the mug, so it has to be somewhere in Ezra's house," said Dad. "He'll find it and feel bad for what he said to you."

"But what if he doesn't find it? What if he broke it and forgot he did?"

Dad shrugged. "Then he'll remember. When he settles down and stops being angry, he'll remember. Either way he'll know the truth."

Roxie leaned back against the wide maple. She took a deep breath. She smelled freshly mown grass, then heard the roar of a lawn mower. Rob was mowing his lawn again. "I know I didn't break anything," she said.

"I believe you," Dad said, smiling. "You always tell the truth."

Roxie glanced at the flower bed as guilt rose up inside her. Mom still thought Chelsea had torn up the flower bed. Roxie bit her bottom lip. And Mom still thought she'd fixed it.

"Mom tells me you helped find Faye today," Dad said, tapping the back of Roxie's hand with his long finger.

Roxie nodded. "My friend Chelsea had a good idea." Her friend Chelsea! That sounded great!

"What was it?" asked Dad.

"She suggested sending Faye to preschool. She says her church has a preschool."

"So it does," said Dad, nodding thoughtfully. "I think your friend Chelsea came up with a winner. We thought of preschool before, but decided against it because we didn't like what we'd heard about it. But a preschool at the church should be just fine. We'll check into it. Faye might be going to school after all." Dad chuckled. "I wish I'd wanted to go to school that much."

"Me too."

"Mom also said you and your friends cleaned Grandma's house today. How'd that go?"

Roxie twisted around, her eyes round. "Oh, Dad! I forgot!" She told him about the missing tools and her call to Sean.

Dad shook his head and muttered something under his breath.

"What'll you do about it?" asked Roxie with her hands clasped at her throat.

"There's really nothing I can do."

Roxie gasped. Had she heard right? "Why not?"

"It's between Grandma and Gabe."

"But the tools are for me!"

Dad nodded. "But Gabe took them."

"Why don't you go to Detroit and take them back?" cried Roxie.

"I couldn't do that."

"But why not?" Roxie wanted to push Dad into his pickup and make him go. What was wrong with him?

"Gabe has them and won't give them up. It's not worth fighting over."

Roxie stared at Dad as if she hadn't heard right. If she were him, she'd take the tools from Gabe and punch him in the nose too. "But Grandma wanted the tools brought here so she could give them to me."

"I'll tell Grandma what happened."

"It'll upset her too much."

"She's a strong lady."

"But, Dad . . . !"

"She'll deal with Gabe. He's been angry for a long time. Maybe the tools will take the edge off his anger."

Roxie's anger turned her face brick-red. "The tools are mine, and I want them!"

"Hey! Don't go sounding like a spoiled brat!" snapped Dad, shaking his long finger at Roxie.

She leaped up. "I thought you'd take care of it! I thought you would!"

"I am going to." Dad jumped up. "I'm going to tell Grandma."

"That's not enough!"

"Watch it, young lady. This is your dad you're talking to."

She bit back another rush of angry words. She didn't want to be punished for being sassy. Just then she noticed his messy overalls and his ugly hat. She had been right about him all along! He wasn't like other dads who solved every problem and who acted normal. She took a deep breath. "Grandma will be upset about the tools."

"She's strong enough to deal with it," said Dad firmly. "You'll see."

"Does that mean I won't ever get the tools?" asked Roxie in a low, tight voice.

"It might. You can always use your mother's."

"It's not the same!" Suddenly she wanted Grandpa's tools more than she'd ever wanted anything—except to go to The Flying W for vacation. With his tools she might be able to be the artist he'd been.

Dad pushed his cap to the back of his head. "Roxie, I'm learning that *things* aren't that important in life. I've worked hard the past twenty years to get *things*. But they didn't bring happiness to any of us. Having each other . . . sharing love . . . playing together . . . those are important." Dad cleared his throat. "And knowing Jesus is the most important thing for all of us."

Roxie stared at Dad in surprise. She'd never heard him say that.

Dad chuckled. "I still feel funny talking about Jesus, but I'm learning. You'll learn too, Roxie."

Would she? She looked down at her sneakers. Right now that wasn't as important to her as getting back Grandpa's tools.

"Do you want to be with me when I tell Grandma about the tools?" asked Dad.

Roxie hesitated, then nodded. Maybe Grandma would ask Dad to take the tools from Uncle Gabe. Dad might listen to *her*.

Roxie walked beside Dad into the living room where Grandma was knitting. The photo of Grandpa wasn't in sight. The room smelled of rose perfume. Grandma looked up with interest.

"Roxann, did you find Ezra's mug?"

Roxie shook her head, then quickly told Grandma the story.

"It'll turn up," said Dad as he sat on the couch across from Grandma. "We have something else to tell you. It's a little disturbing."

Roxie sank to the carpet and leaned against Mom's chair. She suddenly wished she hadn't come.

"What is it?" Grandma's hands grew quiet on

113

the pink-and-white afghan she was knitting. The color drained from her cheeks.

Dad cleared his throat as he twisted his cap in his hands.

Roxie sank lower and wished she could sink right through the carpet. She heard Faye singing in the kitchen.

"What is it?" asked Grandma again, sharper this time.

"Grandpa's tools are gone," said Dad.

Grandma gasped and covered her mouth with her wrinkled hand. "Gone?" she whispered.

"Tell her, Roxie," said Dad.

Taking a deep breath, Roxie told about finding the drawer empty, about searching the house, and about calling Sean.

"Gabe has it," said Dad softly. "He probably wanted something of his dad's . . . especially the tools."

Grandma pressed her lips tightly together. Finally she snapped, "He had no right to take the tools!"

"But he took them," said Dad softly.

"They belong to Roxann," said Grandma firmly.

Roxie sat up. Maybe Grandma would send Dad after them!

"She doesn't need them," said Dad gently. "She can carve with Ilene's."

Grandma sighed heavily. "That's not the point, Burt."

"I know. But that's how it is."

"I suppose you're right." Grandma patted her flushed cheek. "When I'm home again, I'll call Gabe and get it settled."

Roxie sagged back against Mom's chair. Both Dad and Grandma had disappointed her. Maybe she'd have to take care of it herself! Maybe she could call Sean and ask him to send the tools to her. Yes! That's just what she'd do!

The Lies

Roxie waited until everyone was watching TV in the living room, then she ran upstairs and called Sean. This time he answered. Butterflies fluttered in her stomach. The meatballs she'd eaten for dinner suddenly felt like lead weights. "Sean, could you send Grandpa's toolbox to me?"

"That's asking a lot!"

"It is mine, you know."

Sean was quiet a long time. "I know the tools are yours, but I'd get in a lot of trouble if I sent them to you."

"I know. Please, Sean, do it anyway."

"I don't know . . ." Sean's voice trailed off.

Blood pounded in Roxie's ears. "Maybe your dad won't notice they're gone."

"He put them away on a shelf in the garage, so I don't think he plans to use them."

"See!"

"He just wanted them because he said they were rightfully his."

"Will you send them?" Roxie held her breath.

"I don't know."

"Please?"

"All right," said Sean in a low voice. "Tomorrow."

Roxie's heart leaped. "Thanks, Sean. Should I send money to pay you back for postage?"

"No. That's okay. I'll take care of it. I'll send them UPS Overnight, so you should get them in two days."

"Thank you!"

"I just want the tools out of here."

"And I want them!"

"Are you going to use them?" asked Sean.

Roxie twisted the phone cord and looked across the hall toward her room. She'd hidden the mouse she'd carved in the back of her sock drawer. Would she ever carve again? She couldn't tell Sean she wouldn't or he might not send the tools. "I'll use them," she said as she crossed her fingers.

Just then she thought of her special Scripture. If she submitted to God and resisted the devil he'd flee from her.

Impatiently she pushed the verse out of her head. This was not the time to think about it. The tools rightfully belonged to her, and she'd get them back any way she could—even if she never used them. Dad should've done it, but since he didn't she would!

"I'll send them out tomorrow right after Dad goes to the bakery," said Sean with a low laugh. "I wonder how long it'll take him to miss them."

"What'll you tell him when he does?"

"I won't tell him anything. He'd never think I'd do such a thing. He'll think someone walked into the garage and stole them."

Roxie gasped. "Will he call the police?"

"No. He wouldn't want the bother."

Roxie breathed easier. "I have to go now. Thanks, Sean. If I can ever do anything for you, let me know."

"You can trade dads with me."

Roxie's jaw tightened. "You wouldn't want mine either!" She remembered Dad's touch on her cheeks as he'd wiped away her tears. She said a quick good-bye, took a deep breath, and ran downstairs to watch TV so she wouldn't have to think about what she'd done or how she felt about Dad.

Dad glanced over at her as she sat on the floor near Lacy's feet. He smiled, but Roxie couldn't.

The next morning she finished her cereal in silence. The smell of coffee and burned toast hung in the air. Everyone else had eaten. Lacy and Eli had gone to work. Mom and Dad were in the living room with Faye. Grandma had gone back to bed for a little nap, she'd said.

Just then Faye poked her head in the doorway and said, "Roxie, Mom wants you right now."

Roxie's stomach knotted. Had Uncle Gabe learned what Sean planned to do? Had he called? Trembling, Roxie placed her dish in the dishwasher and hurried after Faye into the living room. Mom stood by the front window, and she looked very upset. Roxie looked out the window, and her heart sank. Chelsea was working on the flower bed.

"What is *she* doing out there?" snapped Mom, pointing her finger at Chelsea.

Roxie's mouth felt bone-dry. The milk from her cereal suddenly turned sour in her stomach. "She's working on the flowers," said Roxie in a small voice.

"Your mother told Chelsea never to return," said Dad. "Yet she's out there. Did you tell her she could take care of the flowers again after what she did to them?"

Roxie's head spun. She could never tell the truth now, no matter how badly she wanted to. She had to lie no matter how much Jesus wanted her to tell the truth. "I didn't tell Chelsea to come back," Roxie said hoarsely.

"I'll handle this," said Dad, heading for the front door.

Roxie wanted to catch his hand and stop him, but she let him go. She heard him shout to Chelsea and saw her startled look. Chelsea looked toward the house, and Roxie quickly stepped aside before she saw her. What would Chelsea say? Would she give away the lie?

"I don't like that girl," said Faye with her nose pressed to the window as Dad sent Chelsea home.

"She is not a good friend, Roxie," said Mom sharply. "If she was, she wouldn't take back a job that I'd decided to give to you."

"I know," said Roxie just above a whisper.

Mom waited until Chelsea was out of sight, then she strode from the house and over to the flower bed. She bent down to the plants, then turned and motioned for Roxie to come out.

Slowly Roxie walked over to Mom.

"Roxann Elaine Shoulders, these are not the plants I put in!"

Roxie's face burned with shame.

"How can you tell?" asked Dad, looking down at them.

"By the leaves, of course," said Mom. "Just what do you know about this, Roxie?"

"Well . . ."

"Speak up!" snapped Mom.

"Is it that important?" asked Dad.

"Yes!" Mom's cheeks were bright red, and her eyes snapped with anger as she looked at Roxie. "I'm waiting!"

Roxie's head spun. What could she say? Before she knew the words were there she said, "Some of the other plants died, so I went and bought these. The clerk at the greenhouse said the plants would be nice together." The lies tripped off Roxie's tongue as if she were being totally honest. She was shocked at her own words. How could she lie so easily? "I planted them just the way the clerk said to plant them. They look good. See?"

Mom turned back to the plants and studied them closely.

"They look fine to me," said Dad. He patted Roxie's shoulder. "You managed that very well. I'm proud of you. And so is Mom." He chuckled. "Once she gets over the shock."

Roxie wanted to blurt out the truth, but she wouldn't allow the words past her tight throat.

Finally Mom turned around. She smiled. "I guess they're all right. I'll have a nice surprise when I see them in bloom."

"They'll be beautiful," said Roxie.

"Just don't let Chelsea near them again!" said Mom with a firm shake of her head.

Dad narrowed his eyes. "She won't be. She left in tears."

Roxie groaned. How could she explain all this to Chelsea? How could she let her take the blame? Roxie looked down just as an ant crawled over a piece of grass. She felt lower than the ant. She was the worst person in the whole world! She didn't deserve Chelsea as a friend. And Chelsea probably wouldn't want to be her friend after today.

Roxie stood in the yard as Mom and Dad walked back inside. Dad had said Chelsea left in tears. "What'll I do?" whispered Roxie in anguish.

Just then Gracie ran into the yard and headed right for the flower bed. Roxie yelled, "Gracie! Get away from here!"

Gracie looked back at Roxie, then turned and ran into Chelsea's yard.

"Don't yell at Gracie!" shouted Ezra Menski as he stepped into Roxie's yard.

Roxie didn't have the energy to say anything about Gracie and the flower bed. It wouldn't do any good. Ezra wouldn't believe Gracie would tear up the flowers.

Ezra stopped right in front of Roxie. His face was ashen and his eyes full of anger. "You broke my mug and you stole my money," he said gruffly.

Helplessly she shook her head. "I didn't! What money?"

"I had a one hundred dollar bill and now it's gone!"

"I saw it, but I didn't take it!" She flushed as she remembered she'd been tempted to take it. But she hadn't stolen it! That she knew for sure.

"The money's gone," said Ezra, suddenly sounding and looking very tired.

"I'll show you where it was," said Roxie.

"I put it under the flour canister on the cupboard on the counter," said Ezra.

Roxie nodded. "I know. That's where I saw it. And I put it right back!"

"I looked under the canisters just this morning. It wasn't there."

"But it has to be!"

"It wasn't, I tell you!"

Roxie's shoulders drooped. "I didn't take your money," she said weakly. "And I didn't break your mug."

"I don't believe you."

"Let me look for the mug and the money," she said, feeling very helpless.

"No! I don't want you around me or my house or my dog!"

"I could help you find the money! You probably moved it and then forgot about it."

"I didn't move it," he snapped.

"Just let me look, will you?"

"So you can secretly put the money back? Not on your life!" Ezra turned and walked away, leaning heavily on his cane. At the sidewalk he turned back. "That'll be the end of you in the *King's Kids* work group!" He turned and walked toward home.

Roxie clenched and unclenched her fists. How could so many things go wrong in her life? It just wasn't fair!

Later Roxie flung herself across her bed and

sobbed into her pillow. Finally her tears stopped, and she fell asleep. When she woke up, her mouth felt dry and her tongue seemed to be three sizes bigger. Listlessly she walked to the bathroom, washed her face, drank half a glass of water, then walked slowly back toward her room. She'd stay in her room forever!

Just as she passed the phone it rang. She answered it.

"Roxie, it's Chelsea."

Roxie gasped. "Chelsea!"

"Why didn't you tell your folks the truth about the flower bed?"

"I . . . couldn't."

"You have to! They think *I* ruined the flowers. If they spread that story around, my business could be ruined."

"I'll tell them," said Roxie with her fingers crossed. She had to say something to keep Chelsea as a friend. Roxie closed her eyes tight. Some friend she was! But maybe Chelsea wouldn't learn the truth. "Don't come in our yard until I say it's okay."

"I won't." Chelsea was quiet for a while. "I have some really bad news."

Roxie's stomach knotted. "What?"

"Ezra Menski called and told me you broke his blue mug and stole his hundred dollars."

"But I didn't!" cried Roxie. "Honest!"

"I believe you, Roxie. You don't usually lie."

Roxie's face flamed.

"But we agreed that if anyone complains about *King's Kids'* work or conduct, I'd have to mark that person off the list of workers. Roxie, I have to mark you off. You're no longer a *King's Kid*."

Roxie sank to the floor with a moan. "But I'm innocent! I washed his dishes and cleaned his kitchen, and I did a great job. I didn't break the cup, and I didn't take his money."

"Then we'll have to find a way to prove you didn't," said Chelsea. "I'll get the Best Friends together, and we'll make a plan. Come over today at 4 and we'll talk."

Roxie nodded. "See you at 4."

"And call me when it's safe to come back in your yard."

"I will." Roxie slowly hung up the receiver. She would never tell the truth about the flowers. And Chelsea shouldn't expect her to!

In her room Roxie looked at her clock and sighed heavily. "Four o'clock is a long way off," she muttered. Should she try to get into Ezra's house and find the money and the mug on her own?

12

Ezra Menski

Roxie walked listlessly across the backyard with her head down. The afternoon sun was warm, but the trees shaded the yard and kept her cool. She stopped by the sandbox and kicked one of Faye's trucks. Faye was taking her afternoon nap.

"Roxie, are you all right?"

Roxie looked up with a start. "Hannah!"

"I'm sorry about the trouble with Ezra Menski. I was on my way to see him, and I thought you might like to come along."

Roxie froze. After seeing Ezra this morning she couldn't face him this afternoon.

With her head tilted, Hannah studied Roxie. Hannah's long hair hung over her slender shoulders and touched her peach-colored T-shirt that matched her shorts. "Are you afraid to see him?"

"Ezra thinks I stole his hundred dollar bill," Roxie said. "But I didn't!"

"I believe you," said Hannah. "You wouldn't lie."

Roxie almost choked. Chelsea hadn't told Hannah how she'd lied about the flowers!

"I want to tell Ezra that you wouldn't steal his money," said Hannah as she flipped back her dark hair. "I thought you might want to go with me."

"You could keep him busy while I look around for the money and the mug."

Hannah shook her head. "He's a lot like my granddad was. He'd think you were snooping."

Roxie nodded. "You're right."

"Ezra likes me, and he might listen to me." Hannah chuckled. "He wishes he was Native American like me."

Roxie tugged her white T-shirt over her red flowered shorts. "Why are you helping me?"

Hannah frowned. "Because we're friends!"

"But I don't belong to *King's Kids* any more."

"But you're still a Best Friend. You signed the Pact. To stop being a friend you must tear up the Pact you signed and declare you no long want to be friends."

"I would never do that!" cried Roxie. For the first time she realized just how important being a best friend was. She'd reread the promises she'd made earlier that day, and she'd stick to them no matter what!

Hannah smiled. "Will you go with me?"

Roxie took a deep breath and nodded.

"Let's pray before we go," said Hannah.

Her face red, Roxie glanced around. Would someone see them praying?

Hannah caught Roxie's hand and bowed her head. "Heavenly Father, help us settle this problem with Ezra Menski. Show us where the money and the mug are. Thank You! In Jesus' name, Amen."

Roxie smiled. That hadn't been so bad! Why had she been embarrassed? Hesitantly she said, "How can you be brave enough to pray right where others can see you?"

Hannah shrugged. "Praying is talking to God. I can talk to Him anywhere, just like I can talk to you anywhere." Hannah giggled. "Except God is everywhere, but you can be only in one place at a time."

Roxie hadn't thought about praying being talking to God or to Jesus. So that's why the others could pray whether they were mowing the lawn, running an errand, or swinging in a swing. Since God was everywhere, He could hear them talk to Him wherever they were.

"And God knows everything," said Hannah as they walked toward Ezra's house. "He knows you didn't take the money or break the mug."

Roxie's heart jerked. But that meant He also knew she'd lied about the flowers. And He knew she'd kept the phone message from Mom when

Grandma had first called the day they were going on vacation. He knew everything! She'd thought only she knew the wrong things she'd done. She walked more slowly.

"Roxie, you don't have to be afraid of Ezra. He really is a nice man."

"He doesn't like me."

"Only because you yell at Gracie."

Roxie sighed. "I know. But she keeps trying to tear up our flowers."

"Ezra wants to think she's perfect," said Hannah with a laugh. "But we know better."

A shiver ran down Roxie's spine as they walked onto Ezra's porch.

Hannah stopped at the door, but didn't knock. "I think you should step to the side of the door so he doesn't see you and get mad before I can talk to him."

Roxie agreed and pressed against the side of the house a few feet from the door.

Hannah knocked, and when Ezra opened the door she smiled and said, "Hi. I heard you lost some money."

"That Shoulders girl took it," said Ezra.

"But she says she didn't, and I believe her. I'd like to see where the money was last."

"Oh, all right."

"I brought Roxie with me," said Hannah, reaching over and pulling Roxie's sleeve.

Roxie flushed. "Hi," she whispered.

Ezra scowled, but didn't yell at her. "Come to the kitchen."

Roxie wanted to run away, but she followed Hannah and Ezra through the house to the kitchen. To her surprise it was as clean as she'd left it.

"Show me where the money was," said Hannah.

Ezra lifted the canister. "Right there. But you can see it's gone."

"Wait!" Hannah reached over to the bottom of the canister and tugged. The hundred dollar bill came off in her hand. "It was stuck to the bottom of the canister."

Roxie sighed in relief.

"Well, what do you know!" said Ezra, taking the bill. He set the canister down and turned to Roxie. "I owe you an apology. You didn't take my money."

"No, I didn't," said Roxie. "And I didn't break your mug."

"That's a whole different matter," said Ezra.

"When my granddad was deep in thought he used to carry his coffee cup off and set it down without thinking," said Hannah. "When Grandma asked him where he'd put it, he'd say he never carried it out of the kitchen. She'd look around and sure enough find it in a strange place." Hannah smiled at Ezra. "When you're deep in thought, you might do the same thing."

Ezra rubbed a hand over his cheek. "I don't drink coffee out of that mug."

"But you might've carried it off one time when you were admiring it," said Hannah.

Roxie held her breath.

"You could be right," said Ezra.

Roxie's heart jumped.

"We'll help you look around and see if we can find it," Hannah said.

Ezra nodded. "I don't always spot things when I'm looking."

Roxie followed them from one tidy room to another while Ezra talked about his granddaughter who'd made the mug. In the room Ezra called his den Roxie stopped short beside Ezra's desk. Sitting on Ezra's desk was the dog her grandpa had carved, the dog that looked like Gracie and that Ezra had bought a few years back. Roxie would've known it anywhere. She remembered when Grandpa had carved it. Tears burned her eyes as she remembered watching him take a piece of wood and turn it into a masterpiece.

Ezra turned to Roxie. "That's Mason Potter's work."

"I know," whispered Roxie.

"You can pick it up," said Ezra.

"Who's Mason Potter?" asked Hannah.

"My grandpa who lives in Heaven," said Roxie as she gingerly picked up the brown dog. It looked heavy, but it was lightweight and delicately carved. The hair on the dog looked real. Its nose even looked wet. "I could never do such work," she muttered.

"She carves too," Hannah told Ezra.

"You don't say!" Ezra picked up a wooden mask. "I carved this."

Roxie dragged her eyes off the dog long enough to look at the mask, done just like an American Indian would've carved long ago. The work wasn't as intricate as Grandpa's, but she liked it. "That's nice," she said.

"What do you carve?" asked Ezra.

Roxie shrugged.

"Animals," said Hannah. "I saw a mouse she did. It was good."

Roxie was surprised Hannah remembered and even more surprised that she thought it was good. "I can't do work like this," said Roxie, holding up the dog.

"Not everybody can be a Mason Potter," said Ezra.

Roxie sighed. She knew she'd never be a Mason Potter. Reluctantly she set the dog back on the desk. A piece of drawing paper was flopped over a pile of books. Roxie caught a glimpse of something blue. She lifted the corner of the drawing paper, and there was the blue earthenware mug next to the pile of books. "Look," she said, pointing.

Ezra blushed as he picked up the mug. "Now how did that get in here? I owe you another apology. I'm sorry."

"That's okay," said Roxie. She didn't know what else to say. It was a great relief to have him learn the truth.

"Now you can call Chelsea and tell her," Hannah said as she smiled at Ezra. "We need Roxie in the *King's Kids*."

Ezra nodded. "I'll call and I'll apologize."

"Thanks," said Roxie. She should've been happy enough to leap over the desk, but she wasn't. Thoughts of her lies pressed down on her hard.

They walked back through the house, and Ezra set the mug on the counter. "Just who is the King of the *King's Kids*?" he asked.

"It's Jesus," Hannah said without any hesitation. "He's our King, and we're His kids."

"Is that why you were so sure Roxie didn't take the money or break the cup and then lie about it?" asked Ezra.

Roxie squirmed uncomfortably.

"Yes," said Hannah. "Besides, she's my friend and I know she wouldn't lie or steal."

"I have to go," said Roxie, holding back a sob. She ran out the back door and all the way home. She felt as if everyone could see the dark cloud covering her. She stopped outside her house and looked over in Chelsea's yard. Rob was there. He waved and she waved back, but he didn't run to talk to her like he'd done before. Was he angry at her? Had Chelsea told him what had happened?

Just then Nick Rand rode up to Rob. "Ready to go?" Roxie heard him say to Rob.

Rob got his bike, and they rode away together.

Tears gathered in Roxie's eyes. Would she spend the rest of her life thinking everyone was angry at her because of her guilt?

Slowly Roxie walked into the house. She smelled cookies baking, but she was too upset to go to the kitchen to get one.

Just as she walked past the living room door Grandma called to her.

Roxie hesitated, then stepped into the living room. Grandma sat in the rocker knitting as usual. She wore a rose-colored blouse and blue slacks. Her hair was combed neatly back off her slender face.

"Sit down so I can talk to you, Roxann," said Grandma.

Roxie perched on the very edge of the couch.

"Roxann, I've been praying about what to do about the tools Grandpa wanted you to have."

Roxie gripped her knees with her icy hands.

"And I decided to ask Gabe to send them to you. I have something else of Grandpa's to give to

Gabe that will make him happy. So I called him at the bakery, and he said he'd send them right out."

Roxie's heart sank. Now what was she going to do? She had made more trouble than she could handle.

13

The Truth

Roxie covered her face with her hands and wished she was a million miles away instead of in the living room talking to Grandma.

"Roxann? Roxann, don't you want Grandpa's tools after all?" asked Grandma softly.

Roxie lifted her ashen face. What could she say? "I'll never be a Mason Potter," she whispered.

"Of course not! You have no reason to compete with him. You'll be an artist in your own right. You'll be a Roxann Shoulders! You have a gift—a God-given gift. You can't put it aside just because somebody laughs at you."

Just then Dad strode past the living room door. "I can't believe Chelsea would come in this yard again!"

Roxie leaped up. Chelsea was probably coming to get her for the meeting. "Wait, Dad!"

"I don't want her here," said Dad sharply as he reached to open the door.

Roxie caught his arm and looked up at him with big tears in her eyes. She couldn't take her guilt a minute longer. "Dad, don't yell at her. I lied to you."

Dad stared at her a long time. His face fell, and he looked ready to cry. "You lied to me, Roxie?" he asked in disbelief.

She nodded and hung her head just as Chelsea knocked on the door.

"We'll talk later," said Dad in a strangled voice. "I'll let *you* deal with Chelsea." He walked away as if he had worked fifteen hours without rest.

Roxie wanted to run after him and tell him everything, but she opened the door. "Hi," she said softly.

"Hi." Chelsea smiled. "You didn't come over, so I thought I'd come tell you in person. Ezra Menski called and told me what had happened. You're a *King's Kid* again."

Roxie took a deep breath. She couldn't let her lies go by another minute. "I need to talk to you and Hannah and Kathy."

"They're in my yard right now," said Chelsea.

"Wait here." Roxie poked her head into the living room. "Grandma, I'll be back later and we'll finish talking."

A few minutes later Roxie sat on Chelsea's bed

with the others around her. Tears streamed down Roxie's cheeks, but she didn't care who saw them. She couldn't take the guilt another minute. Silently she asked Jesus to forgive her. Now she had to ask the girls to do the same.

"You'll hate me when I tell you what I did," Roxie said between sniffs.

"We won't," the girls said, shaking their heads.

Roxie bit her lip as she looked at Chelsea. "I lied and got you in trouble with my folks."

"I know," said Chelsea.

Roxie told them exactly what she'd said about the plants and the flower bed. "I am *so* sorry! As soon as I get home I'll tell them the truth. Do you hate me?"

"No," said Chelsea gently.

"We're best friends," said Hannah.

Roxie hadn't believed it was possible, but now she could see they really were her friends. They weren't going to hate her or kick her out just because she'd done bad things. They loved her and had forgiven her. She knew it was because they loved like Jesus did. And she wanted to love that very same way. Suddenly she realized He was real! He was her true Best Friend! She could talk about Him to others just like she talked about Chelsea, Hannah, and Kathy to others. There was nothing to be embarrassed about.

In a low voice she told them about Grandpa's

tools and what she'd done. She even told about keeping Grandma's phone message from Mom the day they were to leave for vacation just so nothing would stop them from going. "If you don't want me for a friend any more, I'll understand," she said, dabbing at her tears.

"We're friends forever," said Kathy, smiling.

"Friends forever," said Hannah and Chelsea.

"If we can help you with anything, we will," said Kathy.

"Thanks," said Roxie. She believed them, and it felt good.

They talked a while longer, then Roxie said, "I have to go home now to talk to Mom and Dad." Her voice broke. "I just hope I can do it."

"You can," said Chelsea with a firm nod. Hannah and Kathy agreed.

"They'll be glad you're telling them everything," said Hannah. "Parents are like that."

Slowly Roxie walked home. The house seemed empty, but finally she found Dad in the basement at his big white steel desk. His hair stood on end, and his face was drawn. The basement smelled like wood and paint from Mom's work area.

"Hi," said Roxie in a little voice. She shivered. Not because the basement was cooler than the rest of the house, but because she was nervous. "I came to talk."

"I think you should," he said hoarsely. He

waved to the old red leather armchair beside his desk. He wore his paint-spattered overalls and a blue work shirt with an ink spot on the pocket.

She sat down and gripped the arms of the chair. She wished he'd pick her up and swing her around and around like he usually did even though it embarrassed her. It wouldn't embarrass her any more. She'd be glad to have him do it! But she could see he wasn't going to swing her around or tell a joke or laugh just because he liked to laugh. She looked down at the concrete floor, then up at him. "I don't know where to start," she finally said.

"With the flowers," said Dad with an impatient wave of his hand. "The flowers."

Roxie hung her head. This was going to be very hard. Silently she prayed for help. At long last she lifted her head and looked Dad squarely in the face. "I was the one who ripped out the plants in the first place. I was angry." She told him exactly what had happened from that point on. "I'm sorry for doing it, and I'm sorry for lying. Please please forgive me."

"I trusted you, Roxie."

"I know."

He brushed a tear from his lashes. "I forgive you."

"Thank you." Roxie wanted to run to him and have him hold her tight, but something in his face kept her on her chair.

"Now tell me about Grandpa's tools," said Dad.

Roxie groaned. She'd planned to tell him, but in her own time and after he was over the shock of what she'd just told him. "I . . . I called . . . Sean."

"So I heard."

She gasped. "Is he in trouble?"

"Yes. Gabe was very angry. Roxie, the good things or the bad things you do affect other people. You should've left the problem about the tools to Grandma like I told you."

"I know," whispered Roxie.

"She would've taken care of it. But now I don't know what'll happen."

"I don't deserve the tools," said Roxie.

"Deserve has nothing to do with it. You tried to handle something that wasn't yours to handle."

"I know," Roxie said again. She hated to see Dad so upset.

"All because you wanted your own way," said Dad, shaking his head as if he couldn't believe it. "What else have you done just because you wanted your own way?"

She laced her fingers together and squirmed uncomfortably. In a small voice she told him about Grandma's phone call the day they were to leave on vacation. "I'm sorry," she whispered.

"Roxie, Jesus says to think of others first," said

Dad as he leaned forward earnestly. "I thought you knew that."

"I didn't," she said. "But I do now."

"I think it's time we learned more about Jesus and what He wants for us," said Dad with a firm nod. "It's time we started reading our Bibles and praying every day."

Roxie nodded. She was surprised, but glad that Dad had thought of it.

Finally Dad stood up. "Now we have to talk to Mom and Grandma."

Roxie sighed heavily.

"I'll be there to help you." Dad slipped an arm around Roxie and pulled her to him. "I'm learning to be like Jesus just like you are. Now we'll learn together as a family."

"Do you really forgive me, Dad?"

"Yes." He kissed the top of her head. "Of course I do."

She sighed in relief as they walked upstairs.

14

Waiting for UPS

Roxie stood in the living room with Dad's arm around her and told Mom and Grandma everything. It was the hardest thing she had ever had to do, next to telling Dad.

Mom brushed at her tears as she walked over to Roxie. "I'm so sorry you had to go through such a bad time," said Mom. She took Roxie in her arms and held her close.

Roxie pushed her face into Mom's neck and clung to her. Mom smelled like herbal shampoo, and she felt soft and good to hug. Roxie had expected her to be angry.

Mom held Roxie away from her and looked into her face. "Honey, when you make a mistake again or when you deliberately do something wrong, deal with it immediately. Go right to Jesus for help. Don't go through the agony you went through this time. Jesus loves you and wants to help you in every situation."

Roxie liked hearing Mom talk that way. "I'm sorry I lied to you and hurt you, Mom. Please forgive me."

"I do! And you forgive me for not being more aware of what was going on with you," said Mom. She kissed Roxie and let her go.

"It's my turn now," said Grandma as she used a tissue on her eyes and nose. "I don't think I've cried this much since . . . since your grandpa died."

Roxie took Grandma's hands in hers. "I'm sorry about Grandpa's tools. I was wrong to have Sean send them."

"But it's done," said Grandma. "Gabe and Sean are coming tomorrow."

"To take the tools back?" asked Roxie stiffly. Could she give them up? Yes! If she had to, she could!

Grandma shook her head. "I have something to give Gabe. I should've done it long ago."

"What is it?" asked Mom.

Grandma sat in the rocker and leaned back as if she had suddenly grown very tired. Mom and Dad sat on the couch, and Roxie sat cross-legged on the floor. Roxie knew Grandma wanted to tell the story in her own sweet time.

"Years ago Mason carved a warrior angel, and he told Gabe he could have it. At the time Gabe didn't want it. He wasn't impressed much with angels . . . Or with Mason's work. After Mason died, Gabe wanted the angel, but I couldn't part with it. It was an amazing piece of work—great detail—wonderfully lifelike. The angel looked ready to go into battle." Grandma brushed her hand over her eyes. "When I called Gabe about the tools, I told him he could take the angel. I suppose in my heart I'm afraid he'll sell it, and it's something I want kept in the family. But that's not for me to consider. Mason wanted Gabe to have it, and I have no right to keep it from him."

Roxie remembered the angel. Every time she'd visited Grandma and Grandpa she'd studied the angel and wondered what battle he was going to fight. Often she'd make up stories about him.

"I wanted that angel too," said Mom with a low sigh.

"I know," said Grandma.

Dad patted Mom's hand.

"I used to pretend the angel was real and was fighting for me," said Mom, smiling. "I'm glad I've learned I have real angels that God has assigned just to watch over me."

"I am too," said Grandma, nodding.

"Gabe won't sell the angel," said Dad, shaking his head.

"I hope not," said Grandma.

"I'll tell him if he wants to sell it, I get first

145

chance," said Mom. "I don't care how much it's worth!"

Roxie scooted back and leaned against Mom's chair and listened to them talk. They had forgotten about her, and she was glad. She'd had more than enough attention to last her a lifetime.

After several minutes Grandma leaned forward and said, "I plan to go home tomorrow. I'm feeling just fine."

"If you're sure," said Mom with a slight frown.

"I want my own bed and my own things about me," said Grandma.

"Then I'll see that you get home," said Dad with a firm nod.

"I'll wait until the UPS truck comes with the tools," said Grandma.

A tingle ran over Roxie. Tomorrow she'd get Grandpa's special carving tools. But would she use them?

The next morning Roxie impatiently waited outdoors for the United Parcel Service truck to come. Mom had said it came by 10 each morning. She often got supplies that way. The others were inside, but Roxie had felt too confined indoors. The sun shone brightly. Robins flew from the maple to the lawn. Across the street Hannah's sisters were playing noisily in their yard.

Suddenly Chelsea, Hannah, and Kathy ran to Roxie. Roxie stared at them in surprise.

"We came to wait with you," said Chelsea.

"Thank you!" cried Roxie.

"We didn't want you to be alone," said Kathy.

"Waiting is hard work," said Hannah.

"It sure is!" Roxie locked her fingers together. "One minute seems an hour long!"

"Let's play a game while we wait," said Chelsea. "We played this in the car when we moved here from Oklahoma."

"What is it?" asked Hannah.

Roxie didn't know if she had the patience for a game right now, but she was thankful for anything that would take her mind off waiting. She sat in a circle with the others on the grass near the driveway.

"It starts like this," said Chelsea. "My grandma decided to take a trip to Texas. She pulled out her suitcase and packed an apple." Chelsea giggled. "You're next, Hannah, because you're sitting beside me. You say what I said, only you have to add something that starts with *b*. We go all the way through the alphabet. If you forget what the rest of us said, you're out."

Hannah giggled. "My grandma decided to take a trip to Texas. She pulled out her suitcase and packed an apple and a begonia."

"A begonia?" cried Chelsea with a wild laugh. "That's a flower! It would get smashed in the suitcase."

"It's just a game," said Hannah, almost falling over with laughter.

Roxie giggled just watching Hannah and Chelsea laugh. It was her turn, and she added a candle. Kathy added a dog, but not Gracie, she said, then laughed harder. They reached the letter *m* before the UPS truck came. The brakes sounded loud in the sudden silence.

Roxie ran to the open truck door and took the package the man held out to her. It was from Sean! "Grandpa's toolbox," she said, trembling so much she almost fell.

"We'll see you later, Roxie," said Chelsea.

"We know you want to go inside with your family," added Kathy.

"Tell us everything later," said Hannah.

Roxie nodded as she said good-bye, then ran into the kitchen where Mom, Dad, and Grandma were having coffee. She handed the box to Grandma. "You open it, and then if you still want to give it to me, you can."

"Thank you," said Grandma with tears in her eyes. Slowly she opened the cardboard box, pulled out the wadded paper packing, and lifted out the wooden toolbox with the lid that had been hand-carved by Grandpa.

Mom caught her breath and gripped Dad's hand.

Roxie trembled, then sank to her chair and locked her hands in her lap.

Lovingly Grandma opened the box. Tools were locked on the inside of the lid and also in place in the box itself. "These tools carved a lot of pleasure for us and others," said Grandma softly.

Blood thundered in Roxie's ears. Could she use Grandpa's tools and create things that would give people pleasure? She bit her lip.

"Here's Grandpa's note to you, Roxann," said Grandma, pulling a folded piece of paper out of the end of the box. She held it to her heart, then slowly handed it to Roxie.

Roxie took it, and the paper seemed to burn her hand. What would Grandpa say to her?

"I'm sorry I didn't give this to you last year," said Grandma, dabbing her eyes with a tissue. "But I couldn't part with the tools or the note. I am truly sorry."

"That's okay, Grandma," whispered Roxie. "Could I read the note alone?"

"Of course," said Grandma. "I must admit I did read it already. I'm sure your mom and dad will want to know what it says."

"We can read it later," said Mom, patting Roxie's arm reassuringly.

"If you decide you want us to be with you while you read it, tell us," said Dad.

Roxie smiled. She didn't want to read it in

front of them in case she started to cry. She excused herself and slowly walked to her bedroom. Tonight she'd be sleeping in her own bed again, and Mom and Dad would be sleeping in theirs. She sank down on the edge of the bed. She noticed it was well-made. Mom made a bed better than anyone she knew. She never left a wrinkle and never had one end of the bedspread touch the floor while the other end was a foot off the floor. The note crinkled in Roxie's hand. She couldn't put off reading it any longer.

Taking a deep breath, Roxie opened the note, then folded it closed again. Her heart raced. She couldn't read it alone! She wanted her best friends with her to help her if she started to cry. She slipped quietly downstairs and out the front door. The girls were sitting in Chelsea's yard.

"Roxie!" they cried, jumping up.

"I have Grandpa's note," she said breathlessly. "I need you with me when I read it." Was that really Roxie Shoulders feeling that way? It was! She really could share her very secret things with her friends. They *were* best friends! Tears sparkled in her eyes, and she didn't care if they saw them. They'd understand.

Chattering encouragement, the girls sat down around Roxie. She opened the letter and read aloud:

"My precious Roxie girl, I love you. You have always been dear to my heart. It's not just because we share the same love for art, but because you took time to tell me what was going on with you. And you always asked about me. You liked hearing about my successes and even my failures. It didn't bore you to listen to me talk about my work. You even laughed at my jokes that nobody else laughed at. Thank you!

"I want you to have my special tools. You have the talent and the gift. Don't let anything or anybody keep you from becoming a great artist. God's Spirit lives in you, so you're never alone. He's your Helper. He'll help you in every area of your life if you allow Him to. Let Him help you with your carvings. Take these tools of mine and make them yours. Someday you can pass them on to a child of yours . . . Or a grandchild. I love you, Roxann Elaine Shoulders. I am proud of you. I'm sorry I couldn't stay around longer to be with you and the rest of my family. But I'm going home to Heaven. Maybe I'll even do some carving there . . . Something special for our Heavenly Father. It makes me happy to think of that. So, Roxie, take up my tools and use them!

"Love, Grandpa."

Roxie pressed the note to her heart and burst into tears. Her friends patted her and murmured encouraging words. Finally she looked up and wiped away her tears.

"I can't carve like Grandpa did," she said brokenly.

"You can!" cried Hannah.

"Remember what he said in there," said Kathy, tapping the note.

"You can't hide the tools away and never use them," said Chelsea. "Your grandpa knew you had talent, and that's why he gave the tools to you. He knew you'd use them. You can do it!"

Roxie listened to them and felt better. She read the letter again, then smiled. She wasn't alone. She had her best friends to encourage her, and she had God to help her. "I can try," she said softly.

Chelsea shook her head. "Not try, Roxie Shoulders. You can do it!"

"You can!" cried Kathy and Hannah.

Roxie burst out laughing. "Yes! With God's help I can do it!"

15

Changes

Roxie waited while Mom read Grandpa's note aloud to Dad. Roxie liked hearing Grandpa's words read aloud.

"It makes me cry," said Mom, blinking to keep back the tears.

"It's a note you'll want to keep forever," said Dad, brushing tears from his lashes.

Roxie nodded. "And I plan to use the tools. I don't care if Jason Woods laughs at everything I carve!"

"Good for you!" Mom hugged Roxie hard. "That's my girl!"

"And mine," said Dad with a chuckle as he hugged them both.

Just then Grandma called from the living room. "They're here. I'll get the door."

Roxie followed Mom and Dad to the living room. A shiver ran down Roxie's spine. Would

Uncle Gabe be mean? Would Sean be mad at her for getting him in trouble? Just then Roxie saw the warrior angel standing on the coffee table. She knelt down to look at it one last time. It was truly a wonderful piece of work. She touched the tip of the sword, the flowing locks of hair, the short robe, and the muscular legs. Could she ever carve so well?

Just then Uncle Gabe, Sean, and Grandma walked in. Uncle Gabe was talking about the drive to Middle Lake. He stopped talking when he saw the angel. He bent down to look at it, then picked it up. Tears moistened his eyes.

Roxie smiled hesitantly at Sean, and he smiled back. He looked sad. She motioned for him to follow her, and they walked to the kitchen. She smelled the coffee Dad had just made in case Uncle Gabe would want a cup.

"I could get you a glass of orange juice," Roxie said.

"No thanks." Sean sat at the table with his head in his hands. His dark hair was combed neatly. He wore a white T-shirt and jeans and new sneakers.

Roxie sat across from him. She hated to see him so sad. Silently she prayed for him. Suddenly a desire to tell him about Jesus rose inside her, surprising her. She hesitated, expecting to feel the usual embarrassment, but none came. She smiled and said, "Sean, Jesus loves you. He wants to take away your sadness and give you joy." Roxie felt as shocked as Sean looked.

"I didn't know you knew about Jesus," said Sean.

"I do."

"Grandpa used to tell me about Him," Sean said wistfully. "I always wanted to have Grandpa pray with me so I could give myself to Jesus, but I didn't have the courage to ask him."

"I'll pray with you," said Roxie, surprising herself even more. She sounded just like her friends!

"I'd like that," said Sean softly.

Roxie took Sean's hand in hers and prayed for him, then led him in a prayer. It was easier than she'd thought. But she wasn't doing it alone—God's Spirit in her was helping her. She squeezed Sean's hand. "It's important to read your Bible every single day. And pray. That's talking to God, and you can do it anywhere at any time."

"Thanks, Roxie," said Sean, smiling.

"You're welcome!" Roxie took a deep breath. "Please forgive me for asking you to send the toolbox. It was wrong of me. I'm sorry I got you in trouble."

Sean shrugged. "It all worked out okay."

Roxie told him about Grandpa's note and how she planned to carve no matter what.

"I read the note," said Sean. "I'm glad I got to."

Several minutes later Uncle Gabe and Sean left, taking the warrior angel with them. Roxie stood in the driveway beside Grandma and waved.

"He won't sell the angel," said Grandma softly. "He promised he wouldn't."

Just then the phone rang, and Roxie raced inside to answer it. It was for Mom, from the Christian Preschool. "I'll get her," said Roxie, putting the phone on hold. She ran to the door and called, "Mom, it's the preschool."

Roxie waited in the kitchen to hear the conversation. She saw the excitement on Mom's face as she picked up the receiver.

Grandma and Dad with Faye on his shoulders walked in. Faye was talking about the warrior angel and asking all kinds of questions about it. That kept Roxie from hearing what Mom was saying on the phone.

Finally Mom hung up and turned to the others. "Good news!" she cried. She tugged Faye off Dad's shoulders and stood her on the floor in front of her. "Faye, how would you like to go to school in September?"

"I *am* going," said Faye with a firm nod.

Roxie laughed along with the others.

"You've been accepted at Christian Preschool," said Mom. "You'll go to school on Monday, Wednesday, and Friday mornings."

"Good," said Faye, looking very smug. She

turned to Roxie. "Now will you teach me how to read?"

"I can try," said Roxie with a laugh. "Come on."

"Wait," said Grandma. "Before you leave, say good-bye to me. I'm going home."

Roxie watched Grandma hug Faye. Grandma looked healthy and strong. The sadness was gone from her eyes. Roxie knew it was because she'd finally stopped wanting Grandpa to come back. She knew he was in Heaven with Jesus.

"Roxann," said Grandma softly as she reached for Roxie, "I love you."

"I love you," whispered Roxie as she hugged Grandma tightly.

"You be sure to show me the first thing you carve with Grandpa's tools," said Grandma.

"I will," said Roxie, and she meant it.

"I just had an excellent idea," said Dad, standing in the middle of the floor with his hands on his hips and his feet far apart. He wore overalls and a blue work shirt.

"What is it?" asked Mom with a laugh.

"You look very smug," said Grandma, grinning.

Roxie smiled at Dad. Whatever it was, it would be exciting.

"Grandma, how would you like to go to the Rocking K Dude Ranch in Wyoming?"

"Flying W," said Roxie, giggling.

"You could ride horses and wear a cowboy hat," said Dad. He winked at Roxie. "But no overalls."

Roxie ran to Dad and hugged him hard. "Wear overalls if you want, Dad! I don't care at all! I love you just the way you are."

Dad kissed Roxie's cheek. "Thanks, cowgirl." He turned back to Grandma. "What do you say? Wyoming, here I come?"

Grandma shrugged as she looked at them. "I never thought about it."

"Say yes!" cried Mom, catching Grandma's hand. "You'll love it!"

"Okay! Yes!" Grandma laughed as she squeezed Mom's hand.

"When can we leave?" asked Roxie.

"In two days," said Dad. "Can we all be ready?"

"Yes!" shouted Roxie for all of them.

Two days later Roxie stood outside the packed station wagon with her best friends. "I'll miss you all," Roxie said.

"We'll miss you!" they said.

"Take good care of the flower beds, Chel," said Roxie.

"I will," said Chelsea with a firm nod.

"And don't let Gracie tear them up!"

"I won't." Chelsea glanced around for Gracie. She wasn't in sight.

"Time to go," called Dad. "Load up, you cowboys and cowgirls!"

Roxie laughed, hugged her best friends, and slipped into the very backseat beside Faye and Lacy. Grandma and Eli sat in the middle seat and Mom and Dad in front. Roxie smelled the grape gum Faye was chewing.

Dad backed slowly out of the driveway. They were finally on their way to The Flying W!

Roxie waved one last time. Chelsea, Hannah, and Kathy waved wildly, jumped up and down, and shouted. Roxie laughed softly. When she returned they'd be there waiting for her and they'd want to hear about every detail of her trip. Best friends were like that!

Roxie settled back in her seat. "I know a good game to play while we travel," she said. "My grandma wanted to go on a trip to Wyoming." Everyone laughed. "And she took out her suitcase and she packed an . . . angel! Okay, Faye, it's your turn. You say what I said and add something that starts with the letter *b*. You know the letter *b*, Faye. I taught it to you last night."

"Bunny!" cried Faye. "She packed a bunny!"

Roxie laughed with the others, then Dad took his turn even though it wasn't really his turn. Roxie didn't care. He was her dad and she loved him.

You are invited to become a *Best Friends Member!*

In becoming a member you'll receive a club membership card with your name on the front and a list of the Best Friends and their favorite Bible verses on the back along with a space for your favorite Scripture. You'll also receive a colorful, 2-inch, specially-made I'M A BEST FRIEND button and a write-up about the author, Hilda Stahl, with her autograph. As a bonus you'll get an occasional newsletter about the upcoming BEST FRIENDS books.

All you need to do is mail your NAME, ADDRESS (printed neatly, please), AGE and $3.00 for postage and handling to:

BEST FRIENDS
P.O. Box 96
Freeport, MI 49325

WELCOME TO THE CLUB!

(Authorized by the author, Hilda Stahl)